Who Killed
Swami Schwartz?

Also by Nora Charles
in Large Print:

Death with an Ocean View

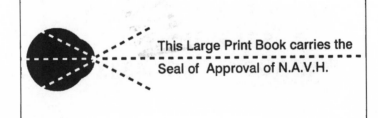

Who Killed Swami Schwartz?

Nora Charles

WHEELER PUBLISHING

Published in 2005 by arrangement with
The Berkley Publishing Group, a division of Penguin Group (USA) Inc.

Wheeler Large Print Cozy Mystery.

The text of this Large Print edition is unabridged.
Other aspects of the book may vary from the original edition.

Set in 16 pt. Plantin by Minnie B. Raven.

Printed in the United States on permanent paper.

Library of Congress Cataloging-in-Publication Data

Charles, Nora.
  Who killed Swami Schwartz? / by Nora Charles.
      p. cm. — (Wheeler Publishing large print cozy mystery.)
    ISBN 1-58724-972-3 (lg. print : sc : alk. paper)
    1. Gurus — Crimes against — Fiction. 2. Women detectives — Fiction. 3. Large type books. I. Title.
  II. Series: Wheeler large print cozy mystery.
  PS3573.A42116W48 2005
    813'.6—dc22   2005002060

To Peggy Hanson
and
Cordelia Benedict,
with thanks

As the Founder/CEO of NAVH, the only national health agency solely devoted to those who, although not totally blind, have an eye disease which could lead to serious visual impairment, I am pleased to recognize Thorndike Press* as one of the leading publishers in the large print field.

Founded in 1954 in San Francisco to prepare large print textbooks for partially seeing children, NAVH became the pioneer and standard setting agency in the preparation of large type.

Today, those publishers who meet our standards carry the prestigious "Seal of Approval" indicating high quality large print. We are delighted that Thorndike Press is one of the publishers whose titles meet these standards. We are also pleased to recognize the significant contribution Thorndike Press is making in this important and growing field.

Lorraine H. Marchi, L.H.D.
Founder/CEO
NAVH

* Thorndike Press encompasses the following imprints: Thorndike, Wheeler, Walker and Large Print Press.

Acknowledgments

IN WASHINGTON, DC —
Many thanks to Pat Sanders who read, edited, and critiqued as I wrote. And to my other Sunday walking pal, Dr. Diane Shrier, for answering my medical questions. Any wrong diagnosis is mine, not Diane's.

I am so grateful to the Rector Lane Irregulars: Donna Andrews, Carla Coupe, Ellen Crosby, Peggy Hanson, Valerie Patterson, Laura Weatherly, and Sandi Wilson.

I thank Susan Kavanagh and Gail Prensky for listening to my writing woes and cheering my small successes.

IN SOUTH FLORIDA —
I couldn't have researched this book without Gloria and Paul Stuart who keep my room ready in their beautiful Boca Raton home, and keep me in a South Florida state of mind.

Thanks to Diane and Dave Dufour for fifteen years of friendship and support.

And thanks to Joyce Sweeney, my writing workshop teacher and mentor.

IN NEW YORK AND NEW JERSEY —
Thanks to Professor Tom Johnson for his
medical knowledge and amusing, on-target
observations.

Thanks to Doria Holland, my dear
friend for over forty years, and Billy
Reckdenwald, my dear son for over forty
years.

And many thanks to my editor, Tom
Colgan, and my agent, Peter Rubie. I
couldn't do this without you guys!

One

"If I subtract ten years and thirty pounds, do you think I'll hear from a few good men?"

Marlene pushed her airbrushed glamour shots toward Kate for her scrutiny. The best would be posted on lastromance.com, a computer-dating site for seniors.

Kate answered her former sister-in-law gingerly. "You might get more responses, but if you lie about your age and weight, what happens when you meet Mr. Right in person?"

Marlene laughed, that raucous, infectious laughter that Kate had enjoyed for almost sixty years. Ballou, Kate's West Highland Terrier, nestled against Marlene's left ankle.

They were sitting on Kate's balcony, watching surfers struggle in a rough-for-South-Florida sea, and creating a brief biography to accompany Marlene's picture.

The warm winter wind seemed to temper the mid-morning sun's rays, but Kate, so fair skinned that she burned, peeled, and freckled in a matter of minutes, had swathed her face and arms in SPF forty sunscreen and plopped a huge straw hat over her short silver hair. Old gray sweatpants covered her long legs.

Marlene wore a red and orange–print tankini, its matching chiffon caftan crumpled up on a nearby chaise, her tanned-to-whole-wheat-toast body begging for more.

"You think the guys aren't lying, too?" Marlene spread Philadelphia Strawberry Light Cream Cheese on a poppy seed bagel.

Kate's eyes followed the trail of tiny black seeds as they slithered down to the floor, leaving miniature polka dots on the ivory tile. She'd earned her "June Cleaver" nickname the hard way: Terminal Tidiness. But as she'd done so often during decades of marriage and motherhood, she bit her tongue. She'd mop the tile after Marlene left.

"Mary Frances had a lively e-mail exchange with a 'sixty-three' year old who bragged about what great shape he was in, then turned out to be over ninety and on a walker." Marlene sipped her tea, frowned, then added another spoonful of sugar.

Since Mary Frances Costello, their Ocean Vista condo neighbor and an ex-nun, was the reigning Broward County

Tango Champion, Kate knew that guy would never have been a match for her.

While Marlene pecked at her laptop's keyboard, Kate, too recently widowed to have any interest in romance, stood and stretched. Her classes at the Palmetto Beach Yoga Institute, complete with meditation techniques, were keeping her mind occupied and her body flexible — she was almost ready to solo on a headstand. Kate's attempts to master that position, while her instructor or another student held her legs up straight, had been exhilarating.

Tonight the institute's founder, Yogi Swami Schwartz, would be honored by the board of directors at Mancini's, Kate's favorite Italian restaurant. Her late husband, Charlie had loved their baked ziti, saying it was every bit as good as Angelo's in Little Italy. Kate had been invited to the party as board member Mary Frances' guest and was looking forward to toasting Swami with champagne. Or maybe not . . . the yogi probably didn't drink.

Kate smiled as she pictured Swami — the man who had changed her life — then easily reached and touched her toes ten times, and sat down.

"The lastromance.com Passion-prompt

is asking me to pick the category that best describes my body type."

Appraising Marlene, most certainly overweight, but with remnants of a former Olympic swimmer's body, still rather firm and strong, Kate weighed her answer. "What are the choices?"

"Slim. Toned & Terrific. Athletic. Pleasingly Plump. Starting a Diet Today."

Feeling like Solomon, Kate nodded. "Well . . . can you select more than one?"

"Yeah . . . I guess." Marlene groaned, then shrugged. "Which ones?"

"Athletic and Pleasingly Plump. You're an appealing combination of those two categories."

Marlene grinned and swung around to her keyboard, causing Ballou to yelp indignantly. "Kate, say that again, slowly, you're talking faster than I can type."

Two

With its light ocean breezes, bright sunshine, and cooler temperature, February in South Florida can seduce a transplanted New Yorker into believing that she lived in paradise, but Kate still had serious reservations about the other eleven months.

On the beach with Ballou, she kicked away a clump of olive green seaweed, then watched a pale yellow moon slowly rising in a Wedgwood sky. Matching her pace, her thoughts meandered from Marlene's dating game to local politics.

In a town still smarting from a scandal redolent of Barry's Washington, Buddy's Providence, and Tammany Hall's New York, Palmetto Beach's current mayor and council had been elected on a reform platform. They were a dour lot. The mayor, a minister, who boasted a LL.B. as well as a D.D., had vowed to return the town to its former glory. His current crusade against lap dance clubs, "sullying the scenery on Federal Highway," waged from his pulpit and while presiding at the Town Hall

13

meetings, had made headlines and had resulted in attendance at both those venues dropping dramatically. Meanwhile, the lap dance clubs continued to thrive.

As an advocate for the homeless, Mary Frances Costello had visited the mayor and reported he'd decorated his office with framed press clippings.

The three councilmen — a butcher, a baker, and a candlestick maker (the latter, a woman, owned a factory over on Powerline Road that produced novelty items, including monogrammed candlesticks) were equally aggressive in asserting how ethically they behaved and in believing their own press releases.

Sometimes Kate found herself yearning for the crooked council she'd helped unseat.

Ballou yanked on the leash, eager ears slightly askew, twisting around to look up beguilingly at his mistress. "Okay," she laughed, "I know I'm a slowpoke."

She moved faster, breathing in the salty, fresh ocean air, letting it smart, then clear her sinuses. Suddenly, overwhelmingly missing her husband, Kate glanced up at the man in the moon's profile and sighed. As if infused with a dose of Charlie Kennedy's NYPD-Homicide-Detective common sense,

14

she decided residents of a town who wanted — and voted — to retain its sleepy charm, shouldn't complain when progress halts and reactionaries rule.

Marlene, Ocean Vista's newly elected condo president, had been making noises about running for town council next year, saying her campaign would promise to put a condom in every pocket. Kate worried that her former sister-in-law might be serious. Maybe flirting through lastromance.com would distract Marlene from her political ambitions.

"Come on, Ballou, we're heading home. I have a dinner party to go to." Though somewhat surprised and more than a little guilty, Kate felt excited about her evening out. It would be fun to wear her blue silk dress again, to pay homage to her yoga instructor, and to feast on Mancini's baked ziti. Oh God! Could she be getting used to life without Charlie? He'd been gone nine months. Time enough to give birth. Time enough to accept death?

Debating whether or not to apply eye shadow and mascara — Marlene had given her a makeover at Neiman's for Christmas — Kate assessed her fine lines, soft jaw, and too-pale skin. Strange how her chestnut hair turning silver had also turned her pink complexion sallow. The portable plastic tray that held all Marlene's magic potions sat in front of her. Sighing, Kate applied more blush and reached for the mascara. Charlie had liked to watch her "fix her face;" she hoped he was still watching. Just in case, she told him, "I'm ready to rock and roll."

A familiar *rat-a-tat-tat* announced Marlene. What did she want? Kate was meeting Mary Frances in five minutes. Not hiding her annoyance, Kate opened the door.

Marlene burst in, waving several computer print-outs. "Can you believe this?" She shoved the papers under Kate's carefully powdered nose. "My picture and bio have been on Last Romance for four hours and I have four responses!"

"Really?" Kate came off as surprised, masking a swift pang of what might be jealousy mixed with awe at Marlene's bravado.

"Of course, three of them are losers. Bachelor number one wanted to know if I had a spare room. Bachelor number two thinks Gore Vidal is a wrestler, and number three still lives with his mother and likes to be tucked in. But this guy," Marlene shuffled the papers and handed one to Kate, "is perfect."

Kate stared at a hazy photo of a man in a tuxedo who looked vaguely like a moon-faced politician her father used to bring home for dinner.

"His grammar is correct, his vocabulary includes words longer than seven letters, and he has season tickets to the Performing Arts Center and the opera."

What about character? Or didn't that count at all?

Marlene read from his e-mail. "I enjoy fine dining, French wine, and Italian films. You sound like a warm, witty woman, whom I would enjoy getting to know and to share my interests with."

Kate nodded. Not many longer-than-seven-letter words in that excerpt. And he'd ended a sentence with a preposition. She'd better watch out, she was bordering on petty.

"Doesn't he sound wonderful?"

Because she loved and didn't want to disappoint her best friend, who'd been married three times and still yearned for another man in her life, Kate said, "Yes."

"We're meeting at the Breakers for brunch tomorrow."

"What? I hope he's treating."

"All according to the Passion-prompt's

17

advice. In broad daylight. Ugh. Who needs that? In a safe place, open to the public. And I'm driving myself up to Palm Beach, so I can leave whenever I want . . . but with this dream-boat, why would I want to leave?"

"Marlene . . ."

"I'm telling you, Kate, this will be a date to die for!"

Three

In addition to her reservations about living in paradise, Kate had reservations about Mary Frances Costello. Conflicting emotions, as her Dr. Phil-obsessed, Harvard pre-law granddaughter would say. God knows she admired the ex-nun's dancing, especially her exotic tango. And with that red hair — probably artificially enhanced, though Kate had never spotted a root — and those emerald eyes and firm figure, the woman would be considered beautiful if she were thirty-five, instead of the "well over sixty" that Marlene insisted she "had to be."

Still, something about Mary Frances bothered Kate. Though she served as an advocate for the homeless, volunteered in a soup kitchen, and seemed both friendly and sincere, Kate couldn't decide if Mary Frances was less than swift or sly as a fox. And, with her bare midriff tops and her bedroom turned into a mirrored dance studio, and her searching for a date online, while "seeing" the only unattached widower in Ocean Vista, Mary Frances' self-

19

promoted chastity irked Kate.

Most puzzling of all, Ballou's tail never wagged when Mary Frances arrived to play cards during the lonely Hearts club's monthly meeting at Kate's apartment. And his body tensed if Mary Frances tried to pet him.

Having lived most of her married life in Rockville Centre, a Nassau County community filled with cops, firemen, and stockbrokers, where she and Charlie had raised their two sons, Kate had never met anyone from Minnesota — and the only former nun she knew well was Sister Jean, her favorite high school teacher who'd introduced her to Graham Greene and then a decade later — post Vatican II — had eloped with a Jesuit from Fordham.

So after nine months, Mary Frances remained an enigma — and, apparently, an innocent, making meaningful dialogue difficult.

As they walked the short distance from Ocean Vista's ornate, faux Roman-and-Greek lobby to Mancini's, whose decor was more Mott Street than myth, Kate let Mary Frances lead the casual conversation, nodding and agreeing with her hero worship of Swami Schwartz. Truth be told, Kate, though too embarrassed to admit it, felt pretty much the same way.

Mancini's, located on Neptune Boulevard, a block from the Atlantic Ocean, abounded with burned-down candles in Chianti bottles, dark paneling, and red and white–check tablecloths. It might have been any Southern Italian restaurant in any New York City neighborhood. At seven p.m., late dining by Palmetto Beach's standards, every table was taken and the small bar to the left of the front door was standing room only.

In his usual Friday-night tribute to Dean Martin, the seventy-something piano player with the really bad rug, was singing "That's Amore" and he sounded a lot like Dino. The twinge of nostalgia sent a shiver of reminiscence through Kate.

Blonde and ponytailed Tiffani Cruz, the perky waitress at Ocean Vista's dining room who drew red hearts over the last "i" on her name tags, moonlighted at Mancini's. Balancing her cocktail-laden tray above her head with one hand, she waved at Kate and Mary Frances with the other. Kate smiled broadly and waved back. The lithe and lovely Tiffani also worked part time and took classes at the Yoga Institute — where she'd helped Kate to *almost* master a head stand — and attended Broward County Community College, "majoring in massage therapy."

Danny Mancini, the restaurant's owner and operator, grabbed Kate's hand mid-air and, with a flourish, kissed it, performing in the manner of a French diplomat rather than a self-proclaimed high school dropout from Brooklyn with reputed mob connections. Tall and very thin, he reminded Kate more of Tony Randall than Tony Soprano. As Mary Frances simpered while Mancini raised her hand to his lips, Kate found herself wishing she had a napkin to wipe away the wet spot he'd left on her wrist.

"Ciao, Bella Katarina." Danny's reedy voice oozed sincerity; however, he'd already turned his attention to Mary Frances. "All in yellow, you look like sunshine, Maria Francesa. Like a tulip in the spring. Like a . . ."

"Is Swami Schwartz here yet?" One more simile and Kate would have screamed. "I think we're running a little late."

"But of course, Bella, though Swami hasn't arrived, I've seated some of the party. Please follow me."

When Mary Frances had invited Kate, she explained that she'd served on the Yoga Institute's board of directors for less than six weeks, but had been taking classes there and helping out with fund-raising for over a year. Swami Schwartz volunteered at the Palmetto Beach Medical Center's Nursing Home, teaching its residents yoga stretches and meditation techniques, and the money Mary Frances and other students solicited was used to buy mats and loose yoga-appropriate garb for those elderly practitioners.

Three well-turned-out people, whom Kate gathered were all board members, sat at a large, round table smack in the middle of the restaurant, apparently awaiting the guest of honor. Kate recognized one of them. Sanjay Patel, her yoga instructor.

The small, slim young man had arrived in the United States from India where he'd been a surgeon and a year later was still waiting to take his Florida State Medical Boards.

A seemingly gentle soul, patient, yet determined, he'd taught his yoga sessions with a quiet energy that made Kate eager to master the positions. Sanjay had introduced her to a special Indian blend of tea, and they often enjoyed a cup and conversation together after class. Kate missed her sons, who both lived in New York, and Sanjay's company made her a little less lonely.

Tonight, dressed all in white, Sanjay Patel looked pure and princely. Kate thought about her pre-law granddaughter, Lauren. Any chance Sanjay could be a fan of Dr. Phil, too?

Nearing the table in Danny Mancini's wake, Mary Frances whispered, "The important-looking gentleman with the silver hair and the two hundred dollar, Palm Beach haircut is Dr. Jack Gallagher, the CEO of the Palmetto Beach Medical Center. So suave. He's a darling man."

Oh, Mary Frances, aren't they all? Kate thought, rather uncharitably.

"And such a humanitarian. His HMO is advertised as the best example of managed care in South Florida."

Kate figured "best HMO" had to be an oxymoron.

"I joined last month and the benefits are wonderful. Why the plan even covers a liver transplant."

Kate had a sudden urge for a double martini.

Mary Frances smiled as Dr. Gallagher stood to greet her.

Sitting next to Gallagher, a glamorous blonde in black — well preserved and doggedly elegant — tugged on his arm. "But you haven't finished telling me about the

Lazarus Society." A pout punctuated her words.

A flash of what? Fear? Anger? clouded the doctor's eyes just before he patted the blonde's shoulder, then greeted Mary Frances with a kiss on each cheek.

"Jack Gallagher," he said, now extending a smooth, large well-manicured hand to Kate. A mid-Atlantic accent honed to perfection. He had to be at least 6'3", all of it toned and covered in Armani, with any visible skin — face and hands — tanned and glowing. And no one could have eyes that blue . . . must be contacts. His features were too rugged to be handsome and he had to be in his late sixties, but his smile, slightly crooked and baring strong white teeth, came across as both over-confident and disarmingly charming.

In the background the piano player crooned, *"Everybody loves somebody sometime."*

A shiver of attraction startled Kate. She hadn't felt anything remotely like this since Charlie had died still clutching the pen he'd used to sign for the condo. The shiver passed, replaced by guilt and a snarly stomach.

She prayed she'd put a Pepcid AC in her purse.

Four

"I'm Dallas Dalton." The blonde had a Texas twang and a diamond necklace that would have crushed a less imposing bosom. "I'm new to Palmetto Beach, but I knew Swami in South Beach and I'm just thrilled to death to have the chance to serve on his little ole board of directors." She drawled "directors" into a paragraph.

Sanjay Patel sprang to his feet, pulled out a chair for Kate, then seated her between himself and Jack Gallagher. Great — surrounded by doctors. Maybe one of them had an antacid in his pocket.

Mary Frances on Sanjay's left leaned across the table to shake hands with Dallas. "Delighted to meet you, Mrs. Dalton. I'm Mary Frances Costello. Aren't you Shane Dalton's widow? I just heard you bought a couple of condos in Ocean Vista."

"Indeed I am, sugar. And call me Dallas. I purchased all five apartments on the right wing of that little ole condominium's top floor and just as soon as the contractors

26

knock down all the walls, and remove those ugly old kitchens, and put in a huge new one, and then redo all five bathrooms in Italian marble, I'm moving in!"

While the ladies were chatting, Kate rummaged in her purse, found the Pepcid AC, popped it in her mouth, and swallowed it neat. Why hadn't Mary Frances mentioned that a famous cowboy star's very rich widow was about to be their new neighbor?

"Are you feeling unwell, Mrs. Kennedy?" Sanjay's soft brown eyes registered concern.

She sighed. "I'm wondering why I'm here. Everyone else seems to be a board member."

"Didn't Miss Costello tell you why you were invited?"

Kate shook her head.

Sanjay smiled. "Like Palmetto Beach, the Yoga Institute is growing. Swami is most impressed with you, Mrs. Kennedy, and he plans to offer you a position on the board."

She'd like to twist Mary Frances into a pretzel position.

"And what about you, sugar?" Realizing a beat late that Dallas Dalton was addressing her, Kate spun her head to the right. "Are you studying under Swami?"

"Why, yes, I am." Kate hesitated. "Although I'm working with Sanjay."

"Well, just among us board members, the amount of hands-on yoga instruction you get from Swami Schwartz seems to be directly connected to the number of zeros in your bank account. I can tell y'all he never let go of my legs."

In the dead silence that followed Dallas's observation, a heavy scent of flowery perfume filled the air, overpowering even Mancini's ever-present smell of garlic.

Jack Gallagher — as if in anticipation of the aroma's owner — was on his feet in a flash, but it was Dallas Dalton who greeted the new arrival, "Well, howdy there, Magnolia. My gracious, aren't you smelling like a gardenia-filled funeral parlor on the last night of a three-day wake?"

Kate knew that Mrs. McFee had endowed the Yoga Institute and served on its board. Though she'd never met the tobacco heiress, she'd seen a portrait of Magnolia, dressed in a blue velvet gown trimmed with ermine, and topped off with a diamond tiara, prominently displayed in the meditation room, and a photograph of her in leotards along with a paragraph praising her philanthropic history graced

28

the institute's brochures.

In person, Magnolia McFee's white hair resembled a cumulus cloud and her thin frame appeared frail. Her portrait and photograph had more than flattered the eighty-seven-year-old woman; tonight the fourth wealthiest woman in America looked like the little old lady she was.

"When are you going to give up that cheap cologne?" The Texas twang grated.

Though Kate had decided Dallas Dalton must be the rudest woman she'd ever met, Magnolia McFee threw back her head and laughed. Color flooded her face, making her instantly appear younger and healthier.

"I see inheriting Shane's millions has done nothing to improve your manners, Dallas, but then what can you expect from a sharecropper's daughter?" Magnolia McFee embraced Jack Gallagher and then took his seat. "Have the waiter rearrange the chairs, Jack. I want to sit next to Dallas, but I want you on my other side." She turned to Kate. "No offense, Miss . . . ?"

"Kate Kennedy. And it's Mrs." She offered her hand, trying to ignore the sickening scent. She'd be delighted to move another seat away. "No offense taken. I gather you and Mrs. Dalton are old friends."

29

Magnolia McFee's pale blue eyes met Kate's. "Old enemies, my dear. So much more fun, don't you think?"

As Kate resettled in her new location, she heard Magnolia McFee ask Dallas Dalton, "So have you joined the Lazarus Society yet? We need fresh blood."

Jack Gallagher made an abrupt and rather rude shift in his chair. His broad shoulders now blocked Kate's view and prevented her from hearing Dallas's response.

A face Kate had seen in the society pages approached the table. Laurence McFee IV, a handsome, if chronically unemployed, soap opera actor, lived in his grandmother's Palm Beach mansion — the society editor always was gushing about how Magnolia's manor rivaled Mar-a-Lago and had been decorated in much finer taste — between acting gigs. Tonight the blond young man wore a navy blazer and a sour expression as he slid into the seat next to Mary Frances.

"Sorry, I had trouble parking the Rolls, Grandmama. And I'm a tad worried." Frown lines formed on his tanned brow. "This is such a dicey neighborhood."

Kate wished she could click her heels and be transported back to her cozy living room where Ballou waited loyally. With the exception of Sanjay and, for the most part, Mary Frances, all the other guests seemed so shallow, so self-serving, so unpleasant. She felt tense and ached to go home. And where was Swami Schwartz?

A deep voice answered her question. "Hello, my friends." The guest of honor took the last available chair, between Laurence McFee IV and Dallas Dalton.

"Rats," Mary Frances whispered, leaning in front of Sanjay Patel. "If Swami had only arrived a minute earlier he'd be sitting next to me."

Kate added Mary Frances to her list of undesirable tablemates.

Five

Swami Schwartz had never hidden his Brooklyn roots. The son of an American father and an East Indian mother, Swami, known as Allen while growing up, took off after high school graduation to find himself in India. He'd stayed there for twelve years practicing yoga and meditation techniques, fasting and praying, then moved to Miami. With the help of a few rich friends like Magnolia McFee, he'd opened the Palmetto Beach Yoga Institute five years ago. At forty-six, he remained reed thin and, despite a pronounced Brooklyn accent, exotically attractive.

Never as attractive as tonight, Kate thought.

Danny Mancini trotted behind Swami carrying a magnum of Moët. "On the house. Nothing's too good for my friend, Swami." Tiffani balanced a sterling silver tray holding eight Waterford flutes. They all, including Danny and Tiffani, toasted Swami with only Sanjay abstaining, hoisting his water glass instead.

Hours later, Kate would recall how quickly attitudes had improved after Swami's arrival. How his charisma captivated her fellow diners and made them smile instead of snipe. How tension evaporated and her stomach felt fine. How with Swami's easy conversation, the mellow music, and the fabulous food, Kate was enjoying herself.

Jack Gallagher had danced with Mary Frances. Laurence McFee led Granny Magnolia in a smooth fox trot. And Swami Schwartz two-stepped all over Kate's new shoes. But she didn't care and, after a second glass of champagne, agreed to serve on the board.

When they'd returned from the smaller-than-her-balcony dance floor, Dallas Dalton was gone. "Ladies room," Sanjay said in answer to Jack Gallagher's questioning the Texan's whereabouts. Yet Kate, while dancing, had observed Sanjay in a close encounter with Tiffani near the espresso machine at the tiny bar and had watched Dallas heading toward the front of the restaurant, away from the rest rooms.

From that moment on, Kate's mental images had moved to fast forward.

Dallas Dalton returned to the table from

the direction of the ladies room. Had she gone out the restaurant's front door, walked around the corner to the parking lot, and reentered through the back door? If so, why? And she'd left her Chanel clutch on the table. Dallas didn't strike Kate as the sort of woman who'd go to the ladies room without her lipstick.

A Baked Alaska presented with flair and flames, both somehow striking Kate as overdone, was followed by an inordinate amount of discussion led by Danny Mancini regarding who wanted cappuccino or espresso and, if espresso, who wanted anisette or Sambucca.

Swami waved away the Baked Alaska and requested tiramisu, saying, "I might as well have my favorite."

Magnolia McFee, passing on dessert, asked Jack Gallagher to dance, as the piano player segued from "I Get a Kick out of You" into "Anything Goes." They managed a more than passable Charleston and by the time they took their seats again, Tiffani was placing a double espresso in front of Swami Schwartz. "Brewed it myself." She spoke softly, in a tone meant to show intimacy.

Kate had swallowed the last of her Baked Alaska and was sipping her cappuccino when Swami, who'd almost chugged his espresso, grimaced, clutched his stomach, and fell face first into the tiramisu.

Dallas Dalton reacted quickly, grabbing his collar and gently lifting Swami's head up. She sniffed, then said, "I smell something . . ."

Removing Dallas's grip on Swami's shirt, Jack Gallagher knelt next to the yogi. "Almonds."

For Kate, sitting next to Magnolia, gardenia still trumped all other scents, and everyone's movements seemed blurred.

"Cyanide!" Dallas Dalton screamed. "Call nine-one-one. Now!"

Magnolia McFee whipped a soft white mask out of her purse and shoved it into the doctor's hand. "Use this while you resuscitate him. You, of all people, know better than to inhale without a filter, Jack."

Danny Mancini fumbled in his breast pocket, then pulled out a cell phone.

Did Magnolia carry a mask with her at all times? Strange? Or convenient?

The older woman clutched her right hand across her heart — looking as if she were about to recite a passionate rendition of the Pledge of Allegiance. She gasped, then said, "Who'd have thought he'd be the first to go?"

35

Though Jack Gallagher worked heroically to revive him, Swami Schwartz was dead.

"So someone has murdered him?" Sanjay Patel might have been talking to himself. He looked shell-shocked.

Mary Frances, who'd been standing, slid back down on her chair, and made the sign of the cross. "Why would anyone want to poison a saint like Swami?"

Turning toward Mary Frances, Kate watched as a smile formed on Laurence McFee's face, quickly fading when he met her eye.

Tiffani Cruz sat in Jack Gallagher's empty chair, weeping wildly. The restaurateur, behind her, spoke to a 911 operator, barking directions, but appearing dazed.

A siren could be heard in the distance.

Just about then Kate reached a frightening conclusion. During all the confusion of the dancers returning to the table, the sugar bowl, the anisette bottle, and the demitasse cups being passed around, and Tiffani pouring espresso while Danny was serving cappuccinos with cute dolphin-shaped stirrers made of brown sugar, each of them had both the means and the opportunity to have poisoned Swami Schwartz.

But who had the motive?

Six

"Any chance Mary Frances killed Swami?" Marlene sounded hopeful. The relationship between Kate's former sister-in-law and the former nun ran from cool to cold to, on occasion, frigid.

They were sitting in Kate's living room with a sleepy Ballou curled in a white furry ball at Marlene's feet, half-on, half-off. Without Charlie Kennedy — who in his widow's opinion had been the sharpest homicide detective ever to grace the NYPD — around to discuss every detail of the yogi's death, Kate had phoned Marlene as soon as she'd returned home, even though by the time the police had finished, it was after midnight. Since Marlene routinely watched Letterman, Kate knew she'd be awake and available to fill in for Charlie.

"Mary Frances idolized the man," Kate said, admitting to herself that she had, too.

Marlene snorted. "Yeah, but from what you're saying about Tiffani's reaction to Swami's demise, her idol had both the proverbial feet of clay and a roving eye for nubile young women. Sounds like the yogi might have been sharing more than a lotus position with Tiffani. Maybe Mary Frances found out and laced his coffee with cyanide."

"I wouldn't count on that." Kate tried to muster a smile, but couldn't.

"Right, our tango champion wouldn't do anything to jeopardize her title. Too bad." Marlene reached down to move Ballou gently off her foot. "If you want to pick my brains in the middle of the night when I should be in bed getting eight hours of beauty sleep in preparation for my date to die for, I require Johnny Walker Black and Lays potato chips."

Kate followed her into the kitchen, putting the kettle on while Marlene poked around in a kitchen cabinet. Like the rest of the apartment, it seemed too bland. Too many neutral tones. Too clean. Too Spartan. Charlie had added color to her decorating as well as to her life.

"Don't you have any onion dip mix?"

"Would you settle for a cup of tea and a piece of crumb cake? I made it myself."

"Oh, Kate, you're still so June Cleaver. Well, when trapped in a TV twilight zone somewhere in the sixties, I can play nice."

Marlene reached into an aluminum canister and pulled out two English Breakfast decaf tea bags. "Here we go."

Kate had bought that canister set at the Macy's Herald Square store in the late sixties while on a shopping spree with her then sister-in-law.

Taking a seat at the table, Marlene gestured toward the cake. "Hey, if I'm giving up booze and dip, give me a hunk of that."

As Kate attempted to cut the cake, her hand shook, scattering crumbs across the place mat.

"Let me do that. Sit down. You're really upset about this Swami Schwartz's death, aren't you?"

"Yes." Kate handed Marlene the knife. "Such a vital man, a truly good man, and his meditation classes have helped me so much. I can't believe he's gone." She wiped a tear with her napkin.

"So who wanted him dead?"

Kate sighed. "According to Detective Carbone that would be Tiffani Cruz."

"Ah. Our old pal, Nick Carbone, is on the case." Marlene cut a slice of cake the size of a shoe and put it on her plate. "Hasn't the Palmetto Beach Police Department put him out to pasture yet?"

This time Kate managed a smile.

"Carbone claims he's South Florida's answer to Lenny Briscoe."

"Hum . . . great cake, Kate. Did you really make it? Or were you just trying to keep me from having a scotch?"

"Of course I made it," Kate said, hoping she'd thrown away the box. "But you wouldn't want to drink so late at night anyway before your big date tomorrow."

"That's true. And I have to get to bed, so let's move this mystery along. If we eliminate you and the dancing nun, I figure one of seven people must have murdered Swami Schwartz. Our new neighbor, Dallas Dalton, for one, who's been tearing up Ocean Vista's entire top floor, making us all hate her before she even moves in. Did you hear she leased a suite of rooms at the Ritz-Carlton in Palm Beach while the world's largest condo unit is being completed?" Not waiting for an answer, Marlene continued, counting on her fingers. "The very rich, very social, very philanthropic Magnolia McFee. Her wastrel grandson, Laurence. That Indian doctor you like so much, Sanjay What's-His-Name. Jack Gallagher — by the way, I heard him interviewed on TV — pompous ass, isn't he? Danny Mancini. He seems like such an old charmer, but I hear he has

40

extremely dangerous friends. Or Detective Carbone's first choice, Tiffani Cruz. And why would our favorite waitress, a walking, talking blonde joke, be his prime suspect?"

"Well, she did brew the espresso *and* serve the double demitasse cup, *and* that cup's dregs did have an almond odor. Nick Carbone latched onto that and wouldn't let go." Remembering, Kate shook her head. "And Tiffani reacted as if she'd been much closer to Swami than any student or part-time employee should have been."

"You said Danny Mancini called nine-one-one. What were all of you doing while waiting for help to arrive?"

Kate nodded, trying to freeze-frame the group's frantic movements. "Dr. Gallagher made a valiant attempt to revive him, but we all knew he was gone before the medics got there. They tried, too. Hooked him up to an IV. The police arrived minutes after the ambulance, but by then there was no question that Swami was dead."

"Tell me about Jack Gallagher's *valiant* attempt. Was the doctor the first one to reach Swami after he'd landed in the tiramisu?"

Kate closed her eyes, trying to recall. "No . . . Dallas Dalton lifted his head up, literally, by the collar, yet with a gentle

41

touch, I thought. Said she smelled some-thing. Then Jack Gallagher pulled her hands away . . . again, gently. I guess the doctor got a whiff, too, because he said, 'Almonds,' then started mouth-to-mouth — wait, no — before he got started, Mag-nolia McFee handed him a mask."

"A mask? Why would she have a mask?"

"Apparently, despite the way she and her grandson danced that lively Charleston, Magnolia McFee is a very sick lady. To quote her: 'My lungs are on their last legs. And my heart's no valentine either. I never know when I'll require resuscitation. Do you think I want some stranger breathing into my mouth without a mask?' "

Marlene grinned. "Not to mention what the good Samaritan might catch from Magnolia."

"Exactly. Or what might have happened to Jack Gallagher if he hadn't been wearing that mask. Sanjay Patel told me that even inhaling cyanide can kill you."

Seven

Jack Gallagher appraised his mahogany deck and the sleek white fifty-foot yawl moored at its far end with smug satisfaction. Hell, he more than deserved all his pretty toys: the custom-made Mercedes, the mansion on the Intercoastal, the Louis XVI furniture — somewhat out of place in a South Florida setting, but what he treasured most of all. He liked to think that Thomas Jefferson might have sat on one of his satin armchairs, supposed to have graced Versailles.

He'd worked hard, too damn hard — racing the clock all of his life — but now time had caught up with him. Though he jogged daily, had the blood pressure of a teenager, could stand on his head lost in meditation for fifteen minutes, and looked a decade younger, he would be turning seventy-nine this spring. And no matter how hard he ran, he couldn't stay far ahead of the grim reaper.

"Cheer up, old man," he said aloud. When had he started talking to himself? "You have more than enough years left to complete your mission."

He turned his face upward, savoring the clear blue sky. Sunshine always lifted his spirits. One of the reasons why he'd decided to move to Palmetto Beach all those years ago.

Yet this morning as the sun's rays peeked through the slats of his blinds, he'd woken up with a dull ache at the back of his skull and not from last night's champagne. His head still hurt. And why shouldn't it? Hadn't his friend died last night? And when Detective Carbone — from whose thick head he'd removed a bullet a few years ago — had said that Horatio Harmon, Palmetto Beach's long-time coroner, was out of town, he'd offered to perform the autopsy today, a procedure that he hadn't done since medical school. Gruesome business. He dreaded it. After tagging the blood samples and sewing the body back together, he'd probably throw up. At least, he hoped events would be in that order.

Friday evening's dinner party had been the start of the worst night of Jack Gallagher's life — and he'd survived some pretty rough nights. He suspected there would be a lot more to come.

His cell phone playing the "Marseillaise"

startled him. He glanced at the caller ID. Magnolia McFee. Damnation! Oh, better answer. She knew he always had his cell phone with him.

"Dr. Gallagher here."

"Oh, my poor darling. What a tragic end for our Swami. And to think, you of all people will be doing his autopsy. You know I plan to lobby Congress against that barbaric procedure. And I swear I didn't sleep a wink last night. Heartbreaking. I ache for you, my dear, dear Jack."

If she weren't the fourth richest woman in America and hadn't endowed both the Yoga Institute and the Medical Center so generously, he would have played the grief card and hung up. Instead, he gritted his teeth and forced a smile into a voice. "You always put others above yourself, Magnolia." Knowing it would drive her crazy, he added. "You need your sleep. I'll prescribe something for you."

"Oh, no. I take too damn much medicine already. What's wrong with you, Jack? You know I want to keep my body as pure as possible."

Had he gotten her mind off Swami? And the autopsy?

"I plan to have a memorial service at my place. A celebration of Swami's life." Her voice caught, but only for a moment. South Florida's most celebrated hostess was on a mission. "When will the body be ready?"

Magnolia, raised in the lap of tobacco luxury in Winston-Salem, had gone through life assuming no one would ever question her decisions. Why fight her? "I'll be doing the autopsy later today and should have the results of the tests and the blood work ready for the police report by tomorrow afternoon. I'll arrange for the undertaker to pick up the body then. How's Tuesday morning for your memorial?"

"I'd like to pick out the casket." Jack could picture Magnolia checking off items on her ever present to-do list. "Is the Adam's Family Mortuary handling things? I'll need to coordinate with them. Swami should look his best. A new Nehru jacket, I think."

"They are. But, Magnolia, there's no need for a jacket. Swami will be cremated."

"Cremated?" He could hear the outrage in her voice. "How can you allow that? As a Christian, don't you believe in the Final Judgment? And the resurrection of the body when it joins its soul for eternity?"

"Swami didn't plan to be murdered. As

46

the executor of his will and his best friend, I'm convinced that, under these totally un-expected circumstances, he would have wanted to be cremated." Jack could feel sweat breaking out all over his body.

"An autopsy and a cremation. Your be-havior belies all that I believe in. All that I thought you believed in, Jack." Magnolia groaned sadly, then made a sniffling noise. "I'm taking this up with the elders at the next Lazarus Society meeting."

"May I remind you, my dear, we are the elders." Not wanting to push the old witch too far, he switched from curt to caring. "Now have a cup of tea, Magnolia, then start planning a great memorial service and an elegant reception. Invite all of the A-list. Think of it as a going away party. I'll bring his ashes in my favorite Indian urn. You know how much Swami always loved your parties."

Eight

Ocean Vista's lobby had been decorated with too much gilt, too much marble, and way too many mirrors for its aging population. The fountain in the center featured a faux alabaster statue of Aphrodite surrounded with Hallmark-card-cute Cupids in some seventies' interior designer's misguided vision of grandeur.

However, the comfortable green couch and several groupings of easy chairs made the lobby a gathering place for gossips. Several sat there now, chatting the fine Saturday morning away.

The front desk, off to the right as Kate and Ballou came out of the elevator, was manned by the miserable Miss Mitford. With her sullen expression firmly in place and a severe black suit covering her thin frame, the sentinel was guarding her post like a U.S. Marine MP guarding his prisoners.

Rather than cross the lobby with Ballou, a violation of the condo's rules, Kate made two quick right turns and exited into the pool area. They'd walk on the beach instead of along A1A. "We're flexible, right, Ballou?"

The Westie yelped eagerly. Kate took that as a yes. Charlie had always insisted that Ballou understood English better than several of his fellow employees at the NYPD.

While she had no real agenda, Kate did have a vague notion she might just check out Mancini's on their morning stroll.

She skirted around the sunbathers sprawled on chaise lounges, all lined up in rows facing east. Nary a head turned as she and Ballou crossed the pool area behind them. Much as she resented Charlie dying, leaving her alone in a retirement place of his choosing, Kate had to admit this was one gorgeous morning. On the beach, palm trees swayed like fat hula dancers in the light breeze. The ocean, white-capped with winter waves — not nearly as high as the summer waves at her beloved Jones Beach — was a Wedgwood blue today, diluting to a hint of aqua in the shallow water. And the sun that Ocean Vista's residents were worshipping deserved nothing less. Big, bright, bold, and beautiful, it sent rays of warmth down Kate's back as she and Ballou trudged north through the sand.

While he preferred woods to water, Ballou seemed delighted to be out for a walk in this glorious weather, investigating the odd dead crab, digging fiercely and spraying sand in his wake.

Uninvited, Swami's death floated into Kate's mind and anchored there, dragging her spirits down, turning the sunshine sour.

What a waste of a wonderful life. A man who'd devoted his time and energy to helping others achieve a healthier body and soul. A man who'd convinced Kate she could move on, cherishing Charlie's memory, and knowing her husband's love would always be with her, by living — or trying to live — in the moment.

Why would anyone want to kill a man like that?

As they neared Neptune Boulevard, Kate marveled at the size of the crowd.

Snowbirds, only in Florida from New Year's to Easter, seemed determined to make the most of their season in the sun. Pale tourists lay on hotel towels, their necks and noses turning red, and it wasn't even ten a.m. Local families toting kids, coolers, and picnic hampers were all set for a long Saturday at the beach. Surfers flirted with pretty girls while waiting to ride a wave. Had she ever been so tanned, so toned, or so young? With her milky-white skin, and her teenage preference for Steinbeck over sports, and her "having been born old" — according to Marlene — Kate decided: No. Never.

Glad to see people milling about on the pier, Kate waved to Herb Wagner, the proprietor of the Neptune Inn as he set up tables for lunch on the restaurant's screened-in porch. Three months ago, he and all the other store owners on the pier had been ready to close, but now with Palmetto Beach's new council's support, their businesses were thriving. That happy thought brought a smile to Kate's face.

Taking a left off the beach at Neptune Boulevard, Kate cleaned up after Ballou, who never did his business in the sand, then deposited the plastic baggie and her Wash & Dri into the large trash can by the public parking lot. Marlene also claimed that Kate had been born obsessive-compulsive. Kate thought of herself as neat: A trait her former sister-in-law had never related to.

Lots of cars and bikes were here today. The Palmetto Beach Library at the far north end of the parking area had a steady stream of young and old passing through its doors. That, too, made Kate smile. She had much more in common with readers than surfers.

"Come on, Ballou, let's do a little snooping." She felt a stir of excitement as they walked west toward Mancini's.

Yellow crime-scene tape in front of the restaurant stopped her in her tracks. What had she expected? Danny Mancini to greet her with a cappuccino and a clue to the killer?

"I guess we can go home now, Dr. Watson." Ballou was pulling her in the direction of the drawbridge, where many more SUVs and convertibles were heading in their direction, then off island.

The door to Mancini's flew open and Tiffani Cruz, followed by a young policeman carrying a ledger and a box of files, came out. The cop nodded at Kate, thanked Tiffani, then walked over to a police car parked a couple of feet away from the restaurant. Some detective. Despite the siren on its roof, Kate hadn't even spotted the blue and white car.

"Mrs. Kennedy, can I talk to you?"

Kate turned away from the young cop, wondering what evidence might be in those files, and saw that Tiffani's eyes were filled with tears.

"Yes, dear." Kate patted Tiffani's hand, noticing the nails were bitten to the quick. Last night, Kate remembered, they'd been blood-red and long enough to stir a drink. Fake, of course. Still she'd never seen Tiffani without them. And the girl wasn't wearing any makeup. Something must be very wrong.

Tiffani yanked her yellow T-shirt down over her belly button in what might be a gesture of respect. Kate's older granddaughter, Lauren, the Harvard pre-law fan of Dr. Phil, always showed some skin between her tops and her bottoms. But her younger sister, Katharine, Kate's namesake and, though she shouldn't admit it, her favorite, kept her stomach covered.

Ballou sniffed at Tiffani's sneakers, then jumped up to sniff and lick her hand — a sure sign of approval.

"I'm so scared, Mrs. Kennedy. I think I'm in big trouble."

Knowing she was being sucked in, Kate went for the bait. After all, the girl was younger than Lauren. "What can I do to help?"

Nine

When the rush of incoming traffic stopped for a red light, Kate led Tiffani across Neptune Boulevard to Dinah's, a Palmetto Beach tradition that was as close to a New York City coffee shop as any restaurant Kate had found in South Florida. Maybe the last restaurant in the United States where she could take Ballou.

Located in the small shopping mall that also housed a bookstore, a drugstore, and a bathing suit shop, Dinah's smelled of freshly baked cornbread and strong coffee.

Kate ordered both. Tiffani only wanted coffee and conversation.

On his best behavior, Ballou lay quietly under the table.

"That Detective Carbone kept me at the restaurant long after you all went home. Me, and Sanjay, and Dr. Gallagher. He kept at me, asking questions over and over about Swami Schwartz and me. You know, personal stuff . . . like was our relationship more than professional."

Kate, dying to know that herself, but

well trained by Charlie, just nodded.

Tiffani was starting to cry. "Honest to God, Mrs. Kennedy, the way that Detective Carbone kept hammering at me last night, it was like so obvious he believed I killed Swami. After what seemed like hours, he asked Dr. Gallagher to do the autopsy, then ordered me and Mr. Mancini to meet him at the restaurant early this morning. Again with the questions. A few minutes ago, Detective Carbone got a phone call, then he and Mr. Mancini took off, leaving me to help that young cop finish packing up the files. And," she sobbed, "Carbone asked me to stop by police headquarters at eleven-thirty. Do you think I'm going to be arrested?" The girl looked terrified.

Three things puzzled Kate: Nick Carbone's seemingly irrational suspicion of Tiffani; why he'd asked Jack Gallagher to perform Swami's autopsy; and where he'd gone with Danny Mancini this morning, leaving his prime suspect behind to gather up what might be evidence. She forced herself to focus on Tiffani's question.

Kate spoke with a lot more conviction than she felt, "Certainly not."

"Mrs. Kennedy, will you please come with me to the police station?" Tiffani's whisper sounded strained. "But we have to stop by the Yoga Institute first. There's something I need to show you before I speak to Detective Carbone."

Need. Kate let the word roll around in her head, deciding when a woman expressed "need" rather than "want," she expected results. If Kate agreed to accompany Tiffani on her morning rounds, would she have to meet her expectations?

"Well, well, fancy running into two of my more charming dinner companions from last night. Neither of you gals spiked the coffee with cyanide this morning, now did you?" Dallas Dalton's twang carried, causing heads to turn. Or maybe her rhinestone cowgirl outfit turned the heads of the diners in the next booth and at the counter.

"Move over, sugar," Dallas said, the white fringe on her jacket swaying as she slid in next to Tiffani. Ballou yelped, but then rearranged himself at Kate's feet. Dallas ignored the little dog, not even acknowledging she'd stepped on his paw. Kate gave him a sympathetic pat.

"My gracious, that cornbread looks as good as my mama's. I think I'll join you all for some postmortem girl talk."

"We have to go soon," Kate said, but her full cup of coffee and untouched food belied her words.

Dallas pointed a French-manicured index finger at her. "So, sugar, whodunit?"

"The name's Kate." Dallas made her lose her appetite. "And I have no idea. Why don't you tell me?"

Could that be a look of respect flashing in Dallas Dalton's big blue eyes?

"Yes — right — Kate. And your last name is Kennedy, if I do recall correctly. Just like my favorite president. Such a tragedy that beautiful man got himself shot in the city I was named after." Dallas flagged one of the waitresses, then gestured toward Kate. "I'll have exactly what she's having, sugar."

Most of the wait staff at Dinah's were women in their late sixties. A few of them — married, widowed or divorced — had worked there part time for decades to get out of the house and meet people, and now considered their steady customers family who couldn't get along without their favorite waitress, but the majority of them worked eight-hour shifts, wearing orthopedic oxfords and support hose, to supplement their Social Security checks.

Madge, the waitress Dallas had addressed, was seventy-two and, indeed, had been at Dinah's for years and loved her customers, but she *needed* — that word again — the money. She'd once told Kate, without a hint of self pity, she'd probably die on the job. Though Dinah's regulars weren't famous movie stars' wealthy widows, they were, for the most part, far better mannered than Dallas Dalton.

"You bet, sugar, in a sec," Madge said sweetly, then walked as slowly as humanly possible over to the sideboard filled with steaming coffee pots. Kate wondered if Madge had ever considered lacing a customer's cup with cyanide.

Tiffani smiled, a wicked little grin, seeming to support a sister waitress's small defiance.

Dallas fixed her baby blue eyes on Kate. With the sun streaming through the window behind her, she looked older than she had in the soft lighting at Mancini's . . . her carefully applied navy eyeliner more noticeable . . . the gray-blue eye shadow slightly smudged. She had creases on her cheeks, but her chin line was firm, her skin pink and healthy, and her smile — much more wicked than Tiffani's — bright. Though past her prime — Kate scolded herself, ashamed of her ageism and sexist thought process — Dallas Dalton was a very pretty woman.

"Is the whodunit question still on the table, Kate?" The twang had acquired a smirk.

Tiffani started, spilling coffee onto her saucer.

"Yes." Kate hoped Tiffani would let Dallas do the talking.

"Did y'all know that Swami's father, David Schwartz, and Danny Mancini grew up in the same section of Brooklyn? That they'd been best buddies back in high school. Went off to World War Two together. I understand they were pretty tough kids. Movable crap games. Fixed fights. All very Damon Runyon. I really loved *Guys and Dolls*, didn't you Kate?"

Sitting next to Dallas, Tiffani looked totally bewildered — and why not? She was much too young to grasp any of Dallas' New York–gangster, musical comedy references.

Without waiting for Kate's review of *Guys and Dolls*, Dallas kept talking, "Even in his golden years, Danny Mancini is quite the gambler. Horses. Y'all know Shane and I loved horses — had our own stable — but we only bet on the Kentucky Derby. For Danny, horse racing is an addiction, not a sport. He owed his bookie three hundred grand. And when he turned to his old pal's son, Swami said no. Now, mind you, he'd already paid off many of Danny's gambling debts. But this time Danny was in real danger of losing the restaurant. He'd already mortgaged his house. If I were a betting woman, I'd wager Danny Mancini killed Swami Schwartz."

Tiffani gasped. "He did insist on pouring the anisette."

Wondering why Dallas was telling them all this, Kate shook her head. "Though Danny had both the means and the opportunity, what would have been his motive? With Swami dead, he couldn't borrow any more money from him."

"Sugar, Danny Mancini is Swami Schwartz's godfather. He's in the yogi's will."

Ten

Marlene hadn't been so excited since she'd lost her virginity. Her heart was dancing to a salsa beat. She turned the air conditioner on full blast. February might be South Florida's coldest month, but hustling around her apartment, bursting with nervous energy and bordering on an anxiety attack, she felt like a hot flash from hell had consumed her body. Sweat seemed to ooze out of the deepest recesses of her soul. And with all the mess — total mess — though Marlene usually preferred to think of the clutter in her apartment as casual disarray, she couldn't find her red patent leather, strappy sandals. The ones with the four-inch heels.

"Think!" Marlene crawled out from under one of the beds in her guest room. "Where did you take them off?" Talking to herself. A sure sign she was crazed. After all, she wasn't seventeen and about to hitchhike down to Rockaway Beach with Tony De Luca to share an illegal beer and a robust round of necking under the boardwalk. A half century had passed; no, flown by.

She was now Marlene Friedman Gorski Kennedy Weiss. Three times a bride. Twice divorced. Once widowed. Well, twice widowed, though Kevin, Charlie Kennedy's twin brother and her second husband, had died long after their divorce. Still, she'd planned and paid for Kevin's funeral, thanks to the generosity of Jack Weiss, her third and last late husband. May he and the Kennedy brothers rest in peace.

Enough with depressing memories. Hell, she might be old, sweaty, and, uh, Rubenesque. But today, she would pull herself together and drive up to the Breakers Hotel in Palm Beach — a far cry from Rockaway Beach — for her first date with a man who composed charmingly romantic e-mails and looked like he enjoyed a good meal. If she could only find her goddamn shoes.

Feeling twenty pounds thinner — her new Lycra tummy tucker working its magic, and her hour-long makeup session leaving a golden glow on her skin, defining her hazel eyes, and creating an illusion of cheek bones — Marlene almost waltzed into the lobby. Only to run into Mary

62

Frances Costello, who was waving a letter and wearing her teacher-knows-best face.

"We have a legal problem."

When the Ocean Vista condo owners had so *wisely* elected Marlene president of the board of directors in a rather distasteful special election that mirrored the town of Palmetto Beach's equally distasteful special election, they'd also *none-too-wisely* voted in the dancing nun as vice-president. Over the last few months, Marlene had been suffering from the results of the electorate's VP decision on a daily basis.

"What now, Mary Frances? I'm on my way to Palm Beach."

"Mrs. Lombardo, on the seventh floor, has complained to the town council about one of Dallas Dalton's king-size whirlpool tubs causing her bathroom ceiling to buckle. A building inspector is on his way. As an eyewitness, I can vouch that Gina Lombardo's ceiling is ready to cave at any moment and she's hopping mad. She just had the bathroom painted and put up new wallpaper. And the fawns are wet."

"Fawns? What the hell are you talking about?"

"Please lower your voice, Mrs. Fried-

63

man." Miss Mitford, the sentinel said, sounding vexed.

"The wallpaper's pattern. Frolicking fawns. That's Gina's bathroom's theme. All the faucets are deer-shaped. Anyway, the fawns were stained by falling wet debris and Gina's going to sue Dallas Dalton." Mary Frances paused, then smirked, and read from the letter she'd been waving around. "She's also suing Ocean Vista's board of directors for agreeing to such an enormous, under-supervised, and completely unethical expansion."

Marlene felt the sweat rising, flooding her face from neck to forehead. She reached into her red patent leather handbag, yanked out a wad of tissues, and then gently patted her cheeks, trying not to smear her makeup. "I have an appointment in Palm Beach."

"You'll have an appointment in court if you don't speak to Gina Lombardo and try to calm her down. She's already hired an attorney and called the *Sun-Sentinel*. Next she'll be appearing on Channel Seven."

Glancing at her watch, Marlene groaned. "Hell's bells. Where is Gina now?"

"Up in Dallas Dalton's spread, screaming at her workmen."

Damn. Since she didn't have his phone number, she couldn't even tell her date-to-die-for that she might be late. Marlene headed for the elevator, calling over her shoulder, "Move it, Mary Frances."

Dallas Dalton owned almost 3,500 square feet, having purchased Ocean Vista's top floor's entire right wing, and turned all five units into a massive apartment, with spectacular views of the pier, the ocean, and downtown Fort Lauderdale.

The whirlpool tub in question was located in what had been a one bedroom unit directly above Gina's condo, but now that one bedroom — along with its living and dining rooms, plus the kitchen and bath — had been remodeled into a resort-size spa.

The workforce that Dallas Dalton had hired, ten men strong, including engineers, electricians, plumbers, and two architects, had allowed Marlene and Mary Frances access to the cavernous apartment.

In an entrance hall the size of Marlene's living room, an irate Gina Lombardo was wagging a finger at a tall guy in designer jeans, while wailing about her ruined wallpaper.

Jeez! Dallas Dalton would need a map to

find the kitchen. "Twenty people could live here with room for guests," Marlene said.

Another older, heavier tall guy, holding a set of blueprints, laughed. "We're imported from Texas, ma'am, we like wide-open spaces." He smiled at Marlene and Mary Frances. "Howdy, ladies, I'm Jeff Jones, the chief engineer."

The designer jeans guy turned out to be the head plumber, also "imported from Texas," and he was assuring Gina Lombardo that he'd solve the problem pronto.

The chief engineer concurred. "Yup. After the plumber fixes the leak, I'll have to reinforce the floor." He smiled at Gina. "And don't you fret, ma'am, Miz Dalton accepts full responsibility for any damage and will take care of all costs incurred by her neighbor down below and the Ocean Vista board." Jeff Jones handed Gina a check. Then he offered another check, made out to Ocean Vista and signed by Dallas Dalton, to Marlene. "Y'all can see the amount has been left blank . . . on both checks . . . just to show our good faith."

Marlene's anger morphed to envy. Being a multimillionaire made life really easy. Then she realized that Dallas' money had solved her problem, too. She took the check and put it in her red handbag. "Thanks."

If she hurried, she'd be on time for her date-to-die-for.

"Mary Frances, let's go." She looked around the ballroom-size living room. No sign of the dancing nun.

The plumber smiled. "I think that pretty little lady went on tour."

"Which way did she head?"

"South, toward the solarium. Now that's really something worth seeing. We put in a skylight and the telescope brings you so close to heaven that you think you're swinging on a star." He gestured left with his thumb. "Go around the circle in the statuary hall outside the kitchen and keep going till you reach the archway. The solarium is off to the east."

Marlene, never noted for her sense of direction, not only couldn't find Mary Frances, she couldn't find her way back to the foyer.

She'd gone round the circle until she felt as if she knew the seven bronze statues — all of dead presidents — on a first name basis. "So Woodrow, where the hell is Mary Frances?"

She decided to search one more time, then try screaming.

At the arch, she turned right and entered a long corridor. Had she taken this route before? No. She'd have remembered that large metal door at the end of the pale yellow hallway.

Would a thick steel door lead to a solarium and a telescope that swept you up to the stars? What would she find behind a door like this? Mary Frances?

Marlene reached for the knob, so icy cold that her fingers smarted. Strange. The door opened. She stepped in. A blast of frigid air almost knocked her off her feet. The temperature had to be way below freezing. Shivering, she glanced around, hearing the heavy door as it closed behind her. Four steel walls. Cables hanging from a steel ceiling. No windows. No furniture. No Mary Frances.

Though she'd been sweating all morning, she felt so cold that her fingers and her toes, peeking out of her red patent leather sandals, hurt. She reached into her matching bag and pulled out her cell phone. Useless. No signal. Damn. She had to get out of here. She spun around and turned the knob. Nothing. She tried again. Oh, God. The door was locked.

Eleven

Kate had heard more than enough from Dallas Dalton. She stood and said, "Tiffani and I have to leave. Enjoy your cornbread."

Back in the almost blinding mid-morning sunshine, Kate readjusted her slouchy hat and big, black sunglasses. If she'd known that Ballou's walk would turn into a marathon morning, she'd have put sunblock and a lipstick in her sweatpants pocket. She certainly wasn't dressed for detective work.

The Westie, happy to be on an extralong outing, pulled on his leash.

"Is your car here?"

"Yes, right over there." Tiffani looked puzzled. "I live way west of Ninety-five, Mrs. Kennedy. And I sure didn't walk across the bridge this morning."

Good Lord. Had Kate become a Palmetto Beach provincial, assuming everyone she knew lived east of the Intercoastal?

Tiffani was pointing across Neptune Boulevard to a faded blue Honda parked in front of the Let's Just Curl Up and Dye hair salon, a few yards away from Mancini's.

Kate had tried and rejected the salon. The owner, a young woman with orange spiked hair, had trimmed Kate's unruly mane, applied a seaweed mousse, then sent her home with silver spikes. Marlene, however, had been having her hair cut and colored there for years — though she traveled off-island to have her nails done.

"Okay, Tiffani. Let's drive for a bit along A1A with the air conditioner on, while you tell me why we *need* to stop at the Yoga Institute to show me something before you meet Detective Carbone at the police station."

Talk about need: The beat up Honda desperately *needed* a good wash. And its interior *needed* a good scrubbing, but first the clutter in the back *needed* to be thrown away. Moving an empty Wendy's bag to the floor, Kate settled into the grimy front seat. Most offensive of all, the car smelled like onions. She rolled down the window.

Tiffani drove south on A1A at a steady pace in the surprisingly light traffic heading toward Fort Lauderdale on this balmy Saturday morning during the height of tourist season.

"So, like what do you want to know,

Mrs. Kennedy?" Tiffani seemed defensive. Did she regret asking for Kate's help?

"I can only give you advice if I know what's bothering you. You said you needed to show me something. What? If I accompany you to the police station, I expect you to tell me and Detective Carbone the truth."

Flashing the right turn signal, Tiffani headed for the Commercial Boulevard Bridge. A half-dozen cars were lined up in front of her, waiting to cross.

"Okay. I'll tell you. But Dallas Dalton delayed us and we have to get to the Yoga Institute before the cops show up with a search warrant. I heard Detective Carbone say that a warrant could take a couple of hours."

Hoping not to show any reaction, Kate merely nodded.

"There's some stuff in the computer that's going to make me look real bad. I swear to you, Mrs. Kennedy, I didn't kill Swami. Why would I? I loved him."

Kate almost whispered her question. "And he didn't love you back?"

"No, he didn't." Tiffani sounded stunned. "I don't get turned down often. I felt hurt . . . and . . . I don't know . . . embarrassed . . . angry. I'd been getting mixed

71

signals from him. I sent him some pretty nasty e-mails after he'd rejected me. And some totally sappy ones before. Combined, they'll add up to a motive for murder."

"Maybe not." June Cleaver at her most reassuring. "Try not to worry." She didn't want Tiffani tampering with evidence. While the girl might be capable of erasing e-mail, Kate didn't think Tiffani could be capable of murder. Carbone must know that, too.

"Swami seemed to like me. A lot. Told me my yoga positions were poetry in motion. Then Mrs. Money Bags, Dallas Dalton, rode into town, offering to serve on the board, to endow the institute, and to fund Swami's research, while crying on his shoulder about her dear, dead husband, Shane. Suddenly Swami became fascinated by a woman old enough to be his mother."

Was Dallas old enough to be Swami's mother? Well, yes. He'd been in his mid-forties. Kate figured that, though well-preserved, Dallas had to be twenty years older than Swami. Of course, Kate could have been his mother, too. And he could have been Tiffani's father.

Tiffani had said something else that intrigued Kate. "What sort of research had Dallas offered to fund?"

The girl shrugged, pulling her visor down. The sun's rays felt more like July than February. The early morning's cool breeze had long vanished. The Honda's air conditioner, obviously as beat up as the car, emitted stale tepid air.

"You got me. Something important, maybe something medical." Tiffani shook her head, her ponytail swinging from left to right. "Magnolia McFee had recently changed her will, leaving the bulk of her estate to Swami Schwartz for a research project that he was way sold on."

"How do you know that?"

"I didn't want to say anything because I really like Magnolia and she adores her useless grandson, but I overheard a screaming match between Swami and that snobby jerk. Laurence kept shouting that he'd see Swami in hell before his family's money ended up supporting some science fiction project."

A woman scorned? A woman in fear of being arrested, attributing a motive for murder to another?

As if reading Kate's mind — or, more likely, her expression — Tiffani said, "If you don't believe me, you can ask Dr. Patel. Sanjay heard them fighting, too. He told me later that Laurence McFee is an angry young man."

Switching gears, Kate said, "Will the Yoga Institute be open this morning?"

"Dr. Patel called me at seven. He was going over there to call all the students and cancel today's classes. Out of respect, you know."

Yes, Kate thought. Or maybe Sanjay Patel had decided that it wouldn't be good for business if the police arrived with a search warrant while the fully packed Saturday classes were in session.

"And Dr. Gallagher's holding a press conference this afternoon to announce that Dr. Patel will be the new director of the Yoga Institute."

Kate wondered if Jack Gallagher's press conference would be scheduled before or after he performed Swami Schwartz's autopsy.

Twelve

Were her fingertips turning blue? Could she have frostbite already? Marlene hopped from one foot to the other trying to stay warm. When exposed to extremely cold conditions a person is supposed to keep moving, right? She could picture her obituary headline: "Woman Freezes to Death in South Florida."

What earthly purpose did this oversized refrigerator serve? How many bloody fur coats could Dallas Dalton own? She banged on the door. Futile. Way too thick. No one could hear her. Surely one of the workmen or Mary Frances would notice she'd gone missing. But what if they just assumed she'd left? The place was so damn big, they might easily believe that.

Why had Ocean Vista's board agreed to let Dallas Dalton gobble up so many units and then allow her to do this hellish renovation? Greed: With Dallas's dough, the board planned on building an indoor garage and remodeling and enlarging the swimming pool.

As condo president, Marlene held herself responsible. Why hadn't she vetoed the motion? Cold guilt blanketed her soul. Would this ice box be her coffin? Even though no one could hear, she screamed.

On her second shriek, the door opened.

"Poor directions, Mrs. Friedman?" The head engineer seemed testy.

"Did you hear me scream?" She couldn't stop shaking. Would she ever be warm again?

"No, ma'am. Nothing can be heard from inside the freezer; its walls are completely soundproof."

"Then how —"

"Your friend, Miss Costello, returned to the foyer alone. I reckoned y'all might have wandered off base." Though he smiled as he held the door open for her, Marlene heard the reproach in his soft southern drawl. Well, hell, she hadn't done anything wrong.

"Are you accusing me of spying, Mr. Jones?" She could be pretty testy, herself.

"Why would you even entertain such a wild idea, ma'am?" Jeff Jones certainly sounded sincere. "I'm just real grateful you're thawing out."

Trailing behind him, she said, "You know damn well that refrigerator is dangerous. Dallas Dalton's asking for trouble. What will she be storing in there?" Marlene wondered if — and why — the building inspector had approved the plans for that room.

Without looking around, Jeff Jones shook his head, but said nothing.

As they approached Mary Frances, who appeared to be flirting with the plumber in the foyer, Jones stopped short, turned, and placed his right hand on Marlene's still cold forearm. "It might be best for both of us, ma'am, if you don't mention your little side excursion to Miz Dalton." Then he gave a quick polite half-bow, like a small boy at dance class, and headed back toward the statuary hall. Or maybe to the freezer.

With the top of her 1958 white Caddy convertible down and the mid-morning sun on her face, a defrosted Marlene was driving up A1A to the Breakers. And, by God, she wouldn't let her fifteen minute delay, even those chilling few minutes in the freezer, ruin her date-to-die-for. The single lane traffic was moving and with any luck — she deserved a break — she might arrive in Palm Beach on time.

She would have taken I-95; however,

highway driving on a Saturday morning in season would totally destroy any shred of serenity — not to mention sanity — that she had left.

As she passed through Delray Beach, the Atlantic on her right and a Mizner mansion on her left, Nat King Cole sang "When I Fall in Love, It Will Be Forever." Marlene smiled, not exactly her theme song, but one lived in hope. She raised the volume on the CD and sang along with Nat.

Having a man in her life was like having a bagel for breakfast. She could get along without one, but why would she want to?

She'd loved all three of her husbands. Truly. If she hadn't, she wouldn't still be looking, would she? Her heart jumped as Nat sang "Mona Lisa." Lying to herself, how devious could she get?

Hell, she'd be looking for a guy even if she'd hated all of her husbands. All of her boyfriends. All of those men who fell into neither category. The truth be told, Marlene *needed* a man in her life. Sometimes the wrong man. Too often, the wrong man.

She shuddered in the warm sun, remembering some of the losers. And the one she'd wanted the most, an insatiable itch that made her betray Kate. A careless four-martini one-night stand, when they'd been very young. And, if possible, he'd felt even guiltier than she had. Adultery is an ugly word, so Marlene Friedman and Charlie Kennedy never spoke it aloud again. And Kate, thank God, had never known. Marlene had lived with the residual scars, marring body and soul, throbbing, unexpectedly, blotting what might have been great days.

Damn it. She was destroying her own serenity. And sanity. She'd have to deal with the guilt, as she'd done for decades. Anything else would only hurt Kate. She loved Kate like a sister. A much longer, far more enduring love than all the others.

Marlene replaced the CD and the memories it had stirred up. Fred Astaire singing Cole Porter always cheered her up.

If Brideshead had been built on the beach, it might have resembled the Breakers. Though she'd been here several times, the approach to one of the most elegant resorts in the world still took Marlene's breath away. The driveway, wide and sweeping. The lovingly nurtured, abundant foliage, wild with color. The manicured lawns on either side, green and lush. In the distance, off to the right, two impeccably outfitted men were playing golf. The weather-beaten shingles in no way detracted from the grand hotel's enduring charm: an architectural marriage of beach cottage and manor house that appeared both imposing and inviting.

In a setting where one almost expected a footman to appear and take your luggage, Marlene settled for valet parking.

Remnants of the Roaring Twenties lingered in the huge, traditionally decorated lobby. Here, again, the Breakers reminded Marlene of a British estate turned into a hotel. Settees and tables grouped in courtly open areas, as well as cozy nooks for private conversations, two fine restaurants, a beautiful bar with an ocean view, smart, upscale shops, and portraits of Henry Flagler, the railroad magnate who'd put Florida on the map. Old Henry could have been the lord of the manor who'd only sold his country house on the condition that he'd always remain on view.

Marlene could picture tea dances, cups spiked with gin, bobbed-hair flappers in short, loose, chiffon dresses dancing the Charleston and flirting with abandon.

It was time to do a little flirting herself.

He'd said he'd be waiting in the north

wing. Well, that covered a lot of territory. Marlene turned left, then right down a long corridor, heading in what she hoped was northeast toward the ocean. After winding up in the freezer, she couldn't count on her sense of direction.

Guests in Brooks Brothers or Burberry sports clothes — lightweight wool, navy blue blazers and white trousers reigned supreme for both men and women — sipped coffee, read the Palm Beach Shiny Sheet, inspected their tennis rackets, or just lounged in the comfortable chairs.

No bathing suits or shorts on parade in this lobby.

Marlene, the lady in red, was the only primary color in sight.

"You must be Marlene Friedman. I'd recognize you anywhere."

She heard him before she saw him. A strong, upbeat voice, coming from her left. She pivoted and watched as a tall, heavyset man, with a kind round face and a broad smile, rose from a club chair off to the side in one of the lobby's cozy corners.

He held out a huge hand. "I'm Harry Archer." His blue eyes twinkled. And he had good teeth.

Best of all, she didn't have to worry about those thirty extra pounds she'd subtracted for her lastromance.com profile. Harry Archer had reduced his weight, too.

A kindred spirit. Kind of sexy. Marlene suddenly felt all warm and toasty. Yes, definitely, a date to die for.

Thirteen

The Palmetto Beach Yoga Institute's pastel rose stucco and charming Spanish courtyard design looked more Boca than Broward.

Sanjay Patel greeted Kate, Tiffani, and Ballou with a shy smile and a pat for the dog, then lowered his eyes. Kate sensed sorrow — genuine — about Swami's death, mixed with another emotion. Could that be fear?

"Look, Sanjay," Tiffani's voice was high-pitched, nervous. "I need to show Mrs. Kennedy something. We'll be in my office. Will you be here for awhile?"

Ballou yelped; Tiffani had stepped on him.

Sanjay stroked the Westie and said, "Oh, yes. I'm waiting for Dr. Gallagher." He turned to Kate. "Has Tiffani told you I'm to be the new director, Mrs. Kennedy?"

Guileless? Or guilty? Kate censured herself. She'd always admired Sanjay, even considered him as a potential date for her granddaughter, for heaven's sake. What was wrong with her?

"Congratulations." She tried to put some warmth into her voice. "Tell me, Sanjay, why is Dr. Gallagher the one to name Swami's replacement? Because he's chairman of the Yoga Institute's board of directors?"

Sanjay seemed embarrassed. "I only learned today that Dr. Gallagher is not only the CEO of the Palmetto Beach Medical Center, where I would like to work after I take the Florida Boards, but he is also the controlling partner in the Yoga Institute. So, in effect, he already is my boss."

Spinning around to confront Tiffani, Kate asked, "Did you know that?"

"You sound like you're accusing me of hiding something, Mrs. Kennedy. Of course, I knew. I keep the records. And the Yoga Institute isn't their only partnership. That's what I wanted to show you."

Kate flinched. "I'm sorry, Tiffani, I didn't —" She stopped, realizing she had no finish, that her mind was in turmoil, that everyone looked guilty.

"If you'll both excuse me, I still have some calls to make to cancel the rest of our afternoon students." With a brief polite nod, Sanjay returned to his small office.

"Are you on my side or what?" Tiffani

had both hands on her hips and a defiant look on her face. She reminded Kate of her younger granddaughter, Katharine, years ago, when she'd been about to throw a temper tantrum.

Kate laughed. "Yes, I am. Now talk to me, Tiffani. And show me the files. I can't help you if I don't know what's going on here."

Tiffani sighed, then her facial muscles relaxed, and she spoke. "Swami and Dr. Gallagher recently formed another corporation. It's called Life Preserver and it's located way out west in an industrial park not far from where I live."

"What does the company do?" Kate took a guess. "Make some sort of safety equipment?"

"I haven't a clue, but it's a totally separate corporation."

"Separate from the Yoga Institute?"

"Yes." Tiffani nodded. "I thought as a board member you might have heard about it."

"I only became a board member last night."

"Right. Maybe none of the board knows." Tiffani twirled the end of her ponytail. "I'm surprised Sanjay didn't."

Kate felt doubt, fear, and a not unpleasant rush of adrenaline. "Let's take a look at those files."

"There's something else." Tiffani had lowered her voice, almost whispering.

As Charlie used to say, there always was. Something more. Something Tiffani really didn't want to share.

Kate waited.

"Come on, I'll show you."

With Ballou at her side, she followed the girl into Swami Schwartz's office. A well-appointed room, with a camel leather sofa, two chocolate-brown leather arm chairs, teak bookcases, a massive teak desk, and an East Indian influence evidenced by the colorful rich fabrics chosen for the drapes and throw pillows. An oval Persian rug covered part of the dark oak floor.

Tiffani pointed to a small desk off in an alcove. "That's my workstation. I'll bring up the Life Preserver file first."

So the "something else" wasn't related to the new corporation? Kate wanted Tiffani to reveal any and all evidence in her own time, but Nick Carbone could be on his way.

With two clicks of the mouse, Tiffani had the Life Preserver Corporation prospectus on the screen. She pointed to the bold, or-nate green script on the cover page.

86

Kate put her prescription sunglasses on.

"See, Mrs. Kennedy, it's out near Power-line Road in a seedy industrial park. I live a couple of blocks from there in a rundown rental complex." She spoke without a trace of self-pity.

Not an address one would associate with the aristocratic doctor whose Medical Center on A1A was state of the art. "How many pages?"

Tiffani clicked again. "Four."

"Quick, print them!" Kate didn't consider this tampering with evidence, after all, they were merely gathering information, not destroying files. Nick Carbone would have equal access to everything.

Kate grabbed the pages, folded them, and stuffed them in her sweatpants pocket. Just in case. "What else do you need to tell me? We don't have much time."

Ballou's ears went up, seemingly on alert, and he barked. Had he heard something? Had the police arrived?

"Now, Tiffani."

The girl clicked again. Another file came up. This one titled "Tantra Workshop."

"What's that?" This time, Kate had no clue. No guess.

Tiffani blushed, color flooding up from neck to forehead. "It's a workshop for a few special yoga students. Swami's private clients." She was whispering again, yet Kate thought she heard a woman scorned. A woman in fear of being arrested.

"Tantra workshops, as the brochures state, provide its participants with an invigorating mix of spirituality and sexuality."

"Just who are these private clients?"

"Well, Magnolia McFee for one."

Good grief, Magnolia was eighty-seven years old. Kate suppressed a giggle.

"And Dallas Dalton has requested a brochure."

"Print it, now!"

Ballou barked loudly as Nick Carbone's rough, angry voice preceded his entrance.

"Who the hell is in there?"

Fourteen

Inside Marlene Friedman's head, Marlene Dietrich was singing, "Falling in Love Again." She'd been named after Dietrich who'd been a glamorous movie star in the late thirties — much admired by Marlene's pregnant mother — and who later worked for the OSS as a double agent during World War II.

Since Kate's mother had called her Katharine, after Hepburn, the two name-sakes had bonded as six-year-olds, the day the Friedmans moved next door to the Nortons. To their parents, how they'd named their daughters was an intriguing coincidence. To the girls, it was destiny. Sixty years later, a shared love of the movies, inherited from their mothers, still fueled their friendship.

Harry leaned across the table and took Marlene's hand in his. "A penny for your thoughts, lovely lady."

He'd drop dead — or, at the very least, drop her hand — if she told him: Dietrich's love song had been the musical accompaniment to a wedding, with Marlene marching down the aisle and Harry waiting at the altar.

Harry's casual banter and hearty appetite had charmed Marlene through a three-course brunch. He loved the same old movies and Broadway shows she did, though, to be honest, she'd generally led the conversation with a comment that he would pick up on. Was he just being agreeable? Or did they really have as much in common as she wanted to believe? She'd been wrong so many times about so many men and, to be sure, she was older now, but was she any wiser?

"Well, I know what I'm thinking." Harry met and held her eyes, not blinking. "I want to know all about you. You're a widow." He shook his head. "Such a shame for a vital woman like you. I mourned my wife for years. Sad to lose the love of your life, isn't it? I'll bet you were a wonderful wife." Harry added another packet of Sweet & Low to his third cup of coffee. "Had you been married before Jack?"

Hell's bells. This was way too soon for that question. Should she tell all now or wait until she knew him better? Maybe she should just mention Kevin. Two husbands seemed fine, but people sometimes reacted strangely when she told them she'd been married three times. So many of her favorite movie stars had to deal with this same problem.

"Yes." She squeezed his hand. "But I'd rather stay in the present. Memories have their place, but not here. Not now. This is our moment." She sounded convincing, even to herself.

"Would you like a glass of champagne?" Harry lifted her hand to his lips. "Suddenly I feel like celebrating."

He waved the waiter over and ordered Moët.

"You're quite right, Marlene. I expect we'll have eternity to discuss our past lives. I tell you what: Let's toast today, and, maybe, if I'm lucky, tomorrow. Could I persuade you to come with me to see a special showing of one of my favorite old movies, *Death Takes a Holiday*?"

"Where?" Like it mattered. She'd have gone alligator wrestling in the Everglades with him.

"At the Boca Raton Resort and Club. A group of my special friends has arranged to show the film there, then we're having a party and discussion afterwards. Should be stimulating." He kissed her hand again.

"Here we go, sir." The waiter had arrived with the champagne.

As they clicked glasses, Harry grinned, the endearing grin of a schoolboy, and said, "Tomorrow is forever. Remember that, Marlene. It's a belief I live by."

Marlene had some hazy recollection of a World War Two movie about Nazis and Hitler's youth called *Tomorrow Is Forever.* Natalie Wood. And Orson Welles? That old flick couldn't possibly have any connection to Harry's philosophy, could it?

"A religious belief?" Damn. Why had she asked that? She wasn't ready for a deep discussion, wanting to keep the conversation as light and happy as the champagne made her feel.

Harry smiled. "Not exactly, though some might say so."

Double damn. Not an enigma. She preferred her men uncomplicated. The only puzzle she wanted in her life was the one in the Sunday *Times.*

Why couldn't they talk about the movie they were going to see tomorrow? Such a posh and pretty place. Marlene couldn't wait. But . . . would Harry turn out to be really weird and spoil everything? How had they segued from *Death Takes a Holiday* to *Tomorrow Is Forever?* Though tomorrow might be forever, if Death took a holiday.

Trying to keep it light, and hoping for the best, she said, "Is your belief sort of like Annie singing about how things will be better tomorrow?"

"Annie who?"

How could a man who professed to love both Broadway shows and movie musicals not have known, immediately, that she'd been referring to Little Orphan Annie?

"Never mind. Tell me more about your group of friends who'll be sponsoring the *Death Takes a Holiday* discussion. Do they all believe tomorrow is forever?" Harry's romance potential was dropping faster than her jaw line.

"Yes. You'll love them. And you'll love learning and coming to accept the possibility of your own immortality."

"Immortality?"

"Yes, my lovely, immortality for those who believe, those who are ready, and prepared to enjoy life everlasting where tomorrow is forever. Come to a meeting, you'll see."

A religious zealot? Somehow she didn't think so.

"What's the name of your group, Harry?"

"The Lazarus Society."

Fifteen

Nick Carbone ordered Tiffani and Kate out of Swami's office. Ballou nipped at his ankles, but the detective wasn't in a playful mood. Paper was spewing out of the printer and, in a bold, large font, "Tantra Workshop" filled the computer's monitor.

Kate probably had "guilty" written across her forehead in equally big, bold letters. In the only saving grace in this compromising situation, she'd stuffed a hard copy of the Life Preserver prospectus file into her sweatpants' pocket.

Standing there, with her straw hat in one hand and her sunglasses in the other, she hoped Nick Carbone had assumed that even though he'd caught her snooping, she had nothing to show for her effort.

God, she must look a fright. Strangely, she felt just as uncomfortable about Carbone catching her minus makeup, her hair uncombed, and her sweat suit looking every bit as grimy as she did.

"Just a minute, Detective, this is my office, too. I'm just doing my job." Surprising Kate, Tiffani was barking back at Nick Carbone. "Why don't you let me finish?"

Snatching up one of the tantra workshop printouts, he glanced at it, then said, "Young lady, you are finished. Take Mrs. Kennedy and get out of here. Wait for me in Sanjay Patel's office."

"But," Tiffani protested.

"Now." Carbone's face contorted, and a vein in his forehead appeared ready to pop.

Without having said a word to Nick Carbone, not even a hello or a good-bye, Kate walked through Swami's office to the door, with a still-muttering Tiffani trailing behind her.

Twenty minutes later Carbone was dropping Kate and Ballou off at Ocean Vista.

Though he'd coldly chastised her in front of Sanjay Patel and Tiffani Cruz, telling her to mind her own business or he'd charge her with obstructing justice, there had been no conversation during the ride from the Yoga Institute, not even during the seemingly endless wait for the Neptune Boulevard Bridge to go down. And, worse, the detective had totally ignored Ballou's obvious delight in seeing him again. Ballou's droopy ears expressed

95

his reaction to the neglect.

Now, as a scowling Carbone drove up the driveway, lined on either side with fat azalea bushes and small palm trees, and braked at her front door, Kate panicked. Tiffani sat weeping softly next to her in the back seat, all bluster gone. Her next stop would be the police station.

Back in the Yoga Institute's reception area, Kate's offer to accompany the waitress there had precipitated the detective's tirade. Tiffani was on her own. Kate desperately wanted to comfort her, to whisper a word of motherly advice about her upcoming interview, but remained silent, afraid that anything she said might make it harder on Tiffani.

Squeezing the girl's hand, Kate opened her door — no gentlemanly manners from the detective today — and, clutching Ballou, stepped out of the car. Carbone took off without a glance in her direction.

Mary Frances huddled in a corner of the lobby, chatting with — or more accurately, at — the recent widower, Joe Sajak, who nodded when necessary. Most Ocean Vista residents considered them to be an item. Kate and Marlene had decided that Joe was only one of several items on Mary

Frances's romance shopping list.

Circling around the far side of the fountain, she approached Aphrodite's statue, praying they wouldn't spot her. As she passed by the cavorting Cupids, thinking she was home free, she heard Mary Frances calling her.

"Kate, Kate, please come over here."

Caught. Damn. And double damn. A few more feet and she'd have made it to the elevator.

"Okay, Ballou, let's go over and see Mary Frances." Kate pushed her damp hair off her face.

"Mrs. Kennedy, what are you thinking?" The sharp rebuke in Miss Mitford's voice made Kate shiver. "You know you shouldn't have that animal in the lobby. And not even on his leash."

"In every adversity there's the seed of an equivalent benefit." Or some such saying. Charlie Kennedy had always been quoting Napoleon Hill. Now Kate could cite Miss Mitford's reprimand and escape from Mary Frances.

She waved at the desk clerk, then looked over at Mary Frances. "Sorry, I'll catch up with you later."

Mary Frances stood and said something to Joe Sajak. Then she started toward

Kate. "You'll want to hear this. Marlene locked herself in Dallas Dalton's freezer. I'll ride up in the elevator with you."

Kate groaned. Mary Frances had to have heard her, but like a fullback carrying the ball, she charged forward.

They met as the elevator door opened. In its harsh fluorescent light, Mary Frances stared at Kate. "Good heavens! Where have you been all morning? You look like death warmed over."

Sixteen

In the shower, with warm water pelting her back and reviving her spirit, and her hair covered in Dove shampoo, Kate reflected on Mary Frances' report about Marlene and that huge ice box she'd stumbled upon in the middle of Dallas Dalton's condo's vast square footage.

What in the world could the Texas glamour girl be planning on freezing in there?

Mary Frances, visibly upset, had confessed to Kate that she was worried about how the Ocean Vista board would answer that question, among many others, to their fellow owners, at the next condo meeting.

As Kate rinsed the shampoo out of her hair, feeling almost like a person again, she wondered if the condo officers, even inadvertently, had allowed Dallas to do something unethical. Or worse, illegal? Some violation of the building code? Could that be why Mary Frances, the board's vice-president, had been so upset?

Stepping out of the shower, Kate smiled.

For sure, Marlene, in the middle of her hot date-to-die-for, wasn't worrying about either ethical or legal concerns.

Kate towel dried her hair, and put on a white, French-terry sweat suit that her daughter-in-law had given her last Christmas. How did everyone seem to know that she'd reached the age of elastic waists and loose tops? Though this smartly cut one sported a designer label. She expected no less from Jennifer, an elegant, style-conscious stockbroker. Slipping into sandals . . . boy could she use a pedicure . . . Kate considered herself dressed. Maybe this South Florida casual living wasn't all bad.

Rescuing the rumpled Life Preserver papers from her pants pocket, she then dumped all of her morning attire into the hamper, and made herself a nice cup of tea.

With Ballou at her side, Kate settled into the beige and white tufted chaise on the balcony, placing the file, the teacup, and a cheese and tomato whole wheat sandwich, liberally spread with both mayo and mustard, on a nearby rattan table.

At high noon on a Saturday, the beach was awash with activity. Since Ocean Vista was the nearest condo to the south side of

the pier, and this was a public beach, lo-
cals, tourists, snow birds, and surfers
waiting in hope of the next big one, had
joined Ocean Vista condo owners on the
wide stretch of white sand beneath her balcony.

Umbrellas of every stripe, folding chairs,
blankets, picnic hampers, and tire tubes
were spread from the Ocean Vista's pool's
gates to the water's edge.

The ocean and the sky were color coor-
dinated in shades of blue, the first ac-
cented with whitecaps, the second with a
few small clouds.

Hungry, she devoured the sandwich,
then returned to the kitchen to fetch a slice
of lemon pound cake and another cup of
tea. Carbs were her favorite food group.
She'd never be able to exist on either the
Atkins or the South Beach diet.

Finally sated, she uncurled the papers,
and read the Life Preserver prospectus.
Then read through a second time, re-
maining confused about what the company
actually did. Medical research to be sure,
with laboratory tests and experiments on
small animals, employing sophisticated
blood work, cells and embryos, all sounding like some sort of cloning, but with
jargon too technical for her to translate

into layman's terms. In addition to what was described as a state-of-the-art lab, there would be a storage area, with its temperature kept below freezing. And the lab would be working on a medical treatment, referenced only as Neuro Option, to perfectly preserve patients. Another of Life Preserver's goals: Vitrifaction. What the devil was that?

Kate got up, went into her bedroom, and looked up the word in her dictionary. "The process of transforming." Well that certainly cleared everything up.

Back on the chaise, she decided to make an appointment with Dr. Jack Gallagher. Something about the gobbledygook in the Life Preserver prospectus scared her. Hard to believe Swami had been a partner in this mysterious company. She wondered if Gallagher's press conference was over. And, though she'd been ordered not to go, she couldn't shake her guilt about not accompanying Tiffani to the police station. Would the girl call when she finished there? If not, Kate would call her.

Two toddlers, walking with a young woman near the shore, caught her eye. For a moment she was back at Jones Beach in the early sixties, Kevin holding one hand, Peter holding the other. A soaking wet, ruggedly handsome Charlie coming out of the ocean and swooping the boys up in his strong arms, then leaning over them and kissing Kate.

Blinking back tears, she closed her eyes.

Seventeen

Charlie kissed her toes. He'd always said she had cute feet and he loved her toes painted in Sunburst Coral polish, peeking out of high strappy heels. "Sexy, Kate. Like your long, chestnut hair."

But she needed a pedicure, didn't she? And her hair wasn't chestnut anymore.

She went back to the image of the red-headed Charlie working his way up from her toes. What she liked best about dreaming was rewinding to the good parts.

A shrill ring awakened her. The sun had gone behind a cloud. And both the sky and ocean were darker shades of blue. A chill in the air made her shiver. She glanced out at the beach. Far fewer people. How long had she been sleeping? What time was it anyway?

The phone rang again. Kate jumped up and went through the sliding glass doors into her sterile off-white living room. She must add some color. Maybe the cornflower blue of the earlier midday sky. On the fourth ring, she grabbed the receiver

104

and said, "Hello," her words thick with sleep.

"Is this Mrs. Kennedy? Kate Kennedy?"

"Yes, it is." She recognized the voice, but still groggy, couldn't connect it to a face. A woman. Older. Southern. Refined.

"Good. This is Magnolia McFee."

Of course. Sweet sound. Steel delivery.

"We're holding a memorial service for our beloved Swami Schwartz at my home, in the garden that faces the sea, on Tuesday morning at eleven. A reception will follow. I trust you'll be joining us, Mrs. Kennedy." No question. A simple declarative sentence.

"Thank you for inviting me. I'd be glad to attend." Marlene would be pea-green not to be invited to this funeral.

"I'm up in Palm Beach. Off A1A, a few houses north of Mar-a-Lago. You can't miss the McFee crest on the front gates." She sighed. "I just don't understand how they ever allowed that dreadful man to buy Marjorie's lovely home and turn it into a private club. The noise carries right over onto my verandah."

Kate, who'd had the former Marjorie Merriweather Post estate pointed out to her by Marlene on more occasions than she could count, said, "I think I know ex-

105

actly where you are."

"Splendid." Magnolia sighed again. "One more thing, Mrs. Kennedy. I'm something of a perfectionist. And we want this memorial to be beautiful. Elegant. Perfect. Swami deserves no less. Don't you agree?"

"Er . . . yes."

"Well, then please come to a rehearsal tomorrow evening at seven. I'm inviting all the board members who were present at Swami's last supper. And his dear friend, our host, Danny Mancini. I feel we should all say a few words at the memorial. With a run-through, we won't be repeating ourselves, now will we? I'll be serving cocktails and a light repast. Formal attire will not be required. My driver will pick you up at six-thirty. And you might take a look at St. Paul's letters to the Corinthians. I believe you'll find inspiration there. Good day, Mrs. Kennedy."

Magnolia hung up, gently, but firmly.

A sharp rap at the front door jarred Kate before she could process her conversation with Magnolia McFee.

Ballou barked. He loved company. Except for Mary Frances.

On her way through the foyer, Kate glanced at the grandfather clock. It actually had belonged to Charlie's grandfather, and was one of the few possessions they'd brought with them from Rockville Centre. Why did so many seniors throw away so much of their past when they moved to Florida? Kate missed her cherrywood four-poster bed almost as much as she missed her bedmate, but Charlie had wanted "a fresh start." Some start. He'd dropped dead at the closing, never sleeping, even for one night, in their new bed.

The condo, all spare lines and neutral colors, had been decorated by her son Peter's long-time partner, Edmund, a plastic surgeon with a flair for interior design. Naturally neat, Kate had adapted to the cool tones and easy-to-clean surroundings, but mourned the warm traditional furnishings she and Charlie had sold or given away before the move.

The clock chimed three times. She'd had a long nap. Thank heavens, she'd put on sunblock. Still, her face felt tight. As tight as her heart.

Suddenly Ballou began barking and leaping against the door. "Who is it?" Old habits died hard. Did she really have to check on the rapper's identity? Could a trespasser triumph over all those locks and manage to get into the building? Well, maybe, but he'd never be able to sneak past Miss Mitford.

"Open the door, Kate." Marlene sounded stressed. She pushed her way in, crying, as she swooped up the little dog, ecstatic to see her.

Strange. Marlene always had been quick to anger, but slow to cry. What happened up in Palm Beach? Or could this be some residual damage from having been locked in the freezer?

"Come in." She kissed Marlene's spotty cheek. "I'll make a fresh pot of tea. It looks as if we're both having a really bad day."

Eighteen

Dr. Jack Gallagher smiled at his reflection in the glass doors on his way into the NBC affiliate station's green room. His on-camera performance had been a smashing success, and the favorable PR had made his drive down to Fort Lauderdale more than worthwhile.

Some of the questions — especially the print reporters' questions — had been rough, almost hitting too close to home, but even today, one of the busiest and most difficult days of his life, he'd fielded them well, employing the charm and grace that had become his trademarks.

All of the newspaper men — the women were never in doubt — would be in his corner, except for that lean and hungry young New York City transplant, Jeff Stein, editor of the *Palmetto Beach Gazette*. How ironic. Jack Gallagher's hometown paper would be the only one to hint at something . . . but the hint would be as vague and unformed as Jeff Stein's wild questions. Vague enough to do no harm to the town's most beloved doctor. In fact, any ugly innuendo might backfire on the editor.

Jack just had to keep going, plowing through this sunny Saturday, a day when he'd violated all that he believed in. A day demanding precision planning. A day utilizing all of his skills as a surgeon. A day draining him dry as he'd performed the autopsy — even more bloody and gross than he'd remembered.

At twenty-one in medical school, a stranger's body had revolted him, but this time around had been unspeakable. He would never have offered to do the procedure if it hadn't been for Swami Schwartz, his long-time friend and business partner. He'd thought of Swami as a son. That's what made all of this so tragic.

With a bit of time before his next appointment, and he sure as hell wasn't relishing that encounter, he deserved a break. Why not leave the car in the Riverside Hotel's parking lot and take a stroll down Las Olas Boulevard? Might put him in a better mood.

The young men lounging in the sidewalk cafés got better-looking every season. Jack smiled at a magnificent creature with dark curly hair, so slim and perfectly-groomed he had to be a model.

Not too many years ago, Dr. Jack Gallagher would have merited a nod or a smile in return. Some small gesture of acknowledgment. But now he'd crossed over into old age and, like so many senior citizens, had become invisible. Younger people never noticed people of a certain age. Looked right through them. He hated being an invisible man.

He supposed age had its compensations, though at the moment he couldn't think of one. All he wanted was to see a glint again in some young admirer's eye. Or the hint of a wicked grin. Some indication that he was still considered attractive. Virile. Appealing.

"Jack, you old sweet thing, fancy running into you." Dallas Dalton was under his nose before he saw her coming. "I've just found the perfect chapeau to wear at Swami's memorial service." She gestured with her left hand, causing the large hat box hanging on her wrist to swing in his direction.

"Hello, Dallas." He had to get away from her. Now.

"Why don't you buy me a Scarlett O'Hara, sugar? This being South Florida, we can't wait for the sun to be over the yardarm. I could really use a drink. Let's go to the bar in the Riverside Hotel. It's nice and dark in there. Cool, too. All these sidewalk cafés are so outdoorsy. And you and I need to talk in private, don't we?"

"I'm really sorry, Dallas, I'll have to take a rain check." He glanced at his watch. "I'm running late as it is."

"Sorry don't cut it, sugar. Not when I'm funding your research to the tune of two million dollars. We need to talk about Thistle!" She thrust the hat box at him, opened her Hermes, pink Birkin — leave it to Dallas to have the "baby" Birkin — and handed him a cell phone. "Cancel your appointment, Doctor."

Jack shook his head, but took the phone.

"I want my horse here with me. No more excuses. I moved to Palmetto Beach so I could be near Thistle. Now I'm here and he's not. You keep stalling me. I want that horse transported to South Florida tomorrow. What's wrong with you? We had a deal. In Texas, we honor our word. And Swami promised. How can you be so cruel?"

"Please, Dallas, lower your voice." Several passersby were staring at them.

"Don't you understand? We never had children. Thistle was like my son. People visit their loved ones who have gone on before them. Even an iceberg like you ought to appreciate how comforting that would be. Well I can't visit Thistle if he's in Arizona and I'm here, can I? And you know I moved here because of Life Preserver. I had to get Thistle out of that situation."

He stared at the cell phone, wishing that Dallas Dalton would disappear. A woman of a certain age . . . all too visible.

"I have contingency plans, Jack." Her face looked hard and cruel in the bright sunlight. "And I've instructed my bankers to stop funding Life Preserver's research program if my horse isn't here by Monday."

Know when to fold, old boy. Don't call her bluff. Cancel your plans.

He dialed Harry Archer.

Nineteen

After decades of dealing with her sister-in-law's real and imagined crises, Kate knew that Marlene would talk in her own good time. To rush her would be futile. And, indeed, once she started talking, it might be difficult to shut her up.

Trouble was best handled in the kitchen, so Kate silently fussed over tea and biscuits, while Marlene sat stonefaced in a white Formica chair, with a faux-leather seat cushion. Why had Kate allowed Edmund to convince her and Charlie that Formica was the way to go in South Florida? The dinette set looked like it belonged in a school cafeteria.

Kate poured boiling water into a china teapot holding two English Breakfast tea bags.

Their silence wasn't uncomfortable, merely anticipatory, like a sotto voce overture promising cymbals and trumpets.

Ballou had given up comforting Marlene and was curled at her feet. She petted him aimlessly, minus her usual enthusiasm.

Since they'd been kids, Kate and Marlene had found comfort in each other's presence: comfort that, on occasion, didn't require conversation.

Reaching for a Social Tea, Marlene finally spoke. "You always were so damn lucky, Kate. Even now with Charlie gone, you've got the boys and those two beautiful granddaughters." Her voice caught in a sob. "And you kept your figure. I'm just a fat old broad with no one to love me."

Whatever Kate had been expecting, it certainly hadn't been anything like this. Had Marlene been drinking? She usually only became maudlin after three martinis. Should Kate cajole her? Or challenge her? Or maybe a little of both.

"Come on, Marlene. Kevin and Peter are your nephews. Didn't Charlie and I name our Kevin after his brother, your husband?" She saw no reason to mention that Kevin had been Marlene's second ex-husband. "Lauren and Katharine are your great-nieces. They both love you. Remember when they played dress up in your evening gowns? And you must know *my* daughter-in-law likes you better than me." That was true. Jennifer, despite her Lowell heritage and her own air of casual entitlement, always lit up when Marlene entered

115

a room. "Edmund adores you. They all do. They're your family. And what about me? You drive me crazy, but I love you, too. And, for the record, when did you start thinking I had a figure worth keeping? You've been telling me since puberty that I'm flat-chested."

Marlene almost smiled, just the barest hint of a twinkle in her red-rimmed eyes.

"Now tell me what happened today to put you in a state of such negative energy." Maybe she could persuade Marlene to join her for a yoga session on the beach. "I have a lot to tell you, too."

The phone rang. Jarring. Obtrusive.

Kate said, "Sorry," then reached for the kitchen extension. "It might be Tiffani. Carbone whisked her off to the police station late this morning. He's convinced she killed Swami."

No question about it. Nothing like a murder investigation and the chance to champion an innocent suspect to chase away the blues. Marlene's eyes lit up.

"Hello."

"Mrs. Kennedy, it's me."

"Tiffani! What happened? I was getting worried."

"Detective Carbone scared the hell out of me. Questions and more questions. He's

116

convinced you and I were up to no good on the computer this morning. But I didn't admit anything. He wants me to take a lie detector test. So I went over to talk to Sanjay. To Dr. Patel. To see if I should hire a lawyer."

"Oh." Kate once again wondered what Tiffani and Sanjay had been discussing at the small bar in Mancini's last night when Dallas Dalton had gone out the front door and then returned through the back door, just prior to Swami's murder.

"Yeah, well, I guess I ought to speak to an attorney. What do you think, Mrs. Kennedy? Can you recommend one?"

Kate hoped she wouldn't be needing one herself. Should she hand the Life Preserver file over to Nick Carbone? Or should she throw it away? Well, certainly not before she showed it to Marlene.

"I'm here with Mrs. Friedman, Tiffani. Why don't you come over and we'll discuss it?"

"I'm working the dinner shift at Ocean Vista tonight. And the early birds start coming in at four-thirty. Can I stop up when I finish? Around nine-thirty?"

"Yes. We'll talk then."

"Thanks, Mrs. K. Bye."

Kate hung up and said, "Let's take our

tea out on the balcony, Marlene. We need a game plan."

Almost everyone had left the beach and the tea had long since turned cold by the time Marlene got around to Harry Archer dropping the Lazarus Society bombshell.

Kate had filled Marlene in on her morning's adventures, including the Life Preserver prospectus heist.

Then she'd ooohed and aaahed in all the appropriate places while Marlene had recounted her visit to Dallas' digs and how she'd ended up locked in the cooler. Both shivered at the thought. They'd discussed at great length why Dallas would have installed a room-size refrigerator, but came up empty. They agreed that Marlene, as condo president, would take the heat. All through the tale, Kate had sensed that Marlene's melancholy mood had not stemmed from her misadventures in Dallas' apartment or even by her fear of Ocean Vista's residents impeaching her. No, Kate had smelled a rat: Marlene's date-to-die-for.

But she hadn't thought he'd be a weirdo as well.

"Up to then, he seemed totally normal? Or had you found him odd even before he started selling immortality?"

"Completely charming. I'm telling you, he seemed perfect. I was falling in love again."

Kate couldn't even count the times she'd heard that song before. "Did you leave then?"

"Of course not. I remembered you saying that Dallas Dalton had been asking Dr. Gallagher about the Lazarus Society last night at Mancini's. I figured that the Society — and possibly, Harry Archer — might have something to do with Swami's murder."

"What did you say to him?"

"I accepted his invitation with pleasure." Marlene seemed a lot perkier. "When opportunity knocks, even a brokenhearted woman must answer. Though I must say all his chatter about immortality — almost like he'd bottled some strange mix of science and spirituality — spooked me."

Kate bit her lip. Could this Harry Archer be dangerous? Or working a scam? But con men weren't usually violent, were they? And how else could she and Marlene find out about this mysterious society?

"Harry gave me this." Marlene reached into her pocket and pulled out a business card. "I didn't want him to know that I wore glasses, so I left them home. Here, you read it, Kate."

"My God, Marlene, Handsome Harry works for Life Preserver!"

Twenty

"Mix me a martini."

Too many afternoons in retirement seemed to segue straight from tea time to cocktail hour. At least investigating Swami Schwartz's murder added purpose to the libations. Marlene was right; though Harry Archer and Jack Gallagher might be dangerous, they couldn't let this opportunity pass them by.

But Kate could delay the cocktail hour. "Why don't you go change your clothes? We can take Ballou for a run on the beach. I'll buy you that martini at the Neptune Inn, then we'll have an early-bird dinner and plan our strategy."

"Okay, but I need a shower." Marlene pulled a strand of platinum hair from her French twist and sniffed it. "And I want to wash away any lingering scent of Harry Archer's cologne. Why don't you walk Ballou? I'll meet you in the lobby at five-thirty."

Feeling almost happy, or if not happy, more alive than she'd felt since Charlie died — though these good moments some-how made her feel disloyal — she said, "While we're having dinner, we can review all the suspects and their motives."

"Not before you buy me that martini."

On the beach, a happy Ballou led his mistress south toward Fort Lauderdale. Usually the Westie turned north toward the Palmetto Beach pier, but as the late af-ternoon sun cast golden shadows over the sand, he'd set off in the other direction with a stride that brooked no argument.

Savoring the salt air, her short hair blowing in the crisp breeze, Kate replayed the conversations she'd had today and tried to process the information she'd gath-ered. Focused on Swami Schwartz's tantra workshop and wondering just what went on during one of those sessions, she started when she heard a shout from be-hind, "Hey, Kate."

She stopped and turned. Ballou yanked on his leash, determined to keep on going. "Just a minute, Ballou."

As Mary Frances drew closer, he barked defensively. No doubt about it, the Westie didn't like her. Well, too bad. He'd just have to mind his manners. "Sit. And be nice." He did, but his unwagging tail and suspicious attitude continued.

"Kate." Her voice sounded tight, strained. "I need to talk to you."

Echoes of Tiffani's *need* to stop at the Yoga Institute. Marlene's *need* to wash that man right out of her hair. Kate's *need* to find Swami's killer.

Ballou yapped, then tugged on his leash again. "Quiet. Sit. Now. I mean it!"

While the dancing ex-nun, wearing a green jogging suit that matched her eyes, looked lovely — Kate couldn't recall Mary Frances ever looking less than lovely — even in the sun's diminished light, she appeared drained.

"Your dog doesn't like me."

"Oh, I wouldn't . . ."

"It's okay. I don't much like him either. He senses that I'm not an animal lover. Most dogs do. Cats don't care." She shrugged. Somehow the gesture had an edge of sadness.

"Okay, Mary Frances, I'm listening." How often had she said that to the boys? To Charlie? Her granddaughters hadn't wanted to confide. At least, not lately. She missed Lauren and Katharine. And she missed being an on-duty wife and mother. Missed being asked to listen. She felt as if she'd been laid off from a forty-five year

123

career and her skills were getting rusty.

The tension lines around Mary Frances's mouth relaxed. "I don't want to go to Detective Carbone. Not yet." The strain on her face may have eased, but she still sounded frazzled.

Kate shushed Ballou, shifted his pooper-scooper from her right to left hand, then reached out and touched her arm.

Mary Frances sighed. "Even discussing this with you, I feel disloyal to Swami. I'd considered him to be the finest human being I ever knew." Kate caught the past tense in the ex-nun's assessment of the yogi. "I have so many questions."

Following her long-proven formula, Kate nodded, saying nothing.

"I heard Sanjay accuse Swami of toying with Tiffani. He'd raised his voice — he never does, you know — shouting, 'She's an innocent girl and you're old enough to be her father.' They had no idea I was right outside the office." Who knew so much eavesdropping had gone on at the Yoga Institute? "It's just awful, Kate. I've tried to erase the accusation from my mind, tried to pretend that Sanjay, who has an obvious crush on Tiffani — and, I assure you if she's an innocent, I'm Mother Teresa — had to be mistaken. Now," her voice cracked, "now I wonder if Swami had been involved with Tiffani and Sanjay had been jealous enough to murder him."

"Awful," Kate agreed, thinking if Mary Frances had a *need* to talk, carpe diem. Funny how Latin phrases from her high school days lingered in her head fifty years later, helping her solve crossword puzzles and maybe catch a killer. She would seize the day. And the moment. Get to Mary Frances while she seemed so open to discussing the yogi's murder. "Talking about Swami and sex," Kate watched Mary Frances flinch, "what do you think about those Tantra Workshops?"

"How do you know about the workshops?" Even Judi Dench couldn't have feigned the shock on Mary Frances' face.

Kate didn't want to admit to her computer caper . . . and didn't want to lie either. "I sort of stumbled onto some information. Seemed rather sleazy."

Her explanation sounded weak even to herself, but Mary Frances jumped right in. "Sleazy, indeed. Swami's sideline went against all decency. Tantra wasn't even part of my vocabulary until Dallas Dalton told me about the workshops. She urged me to join, said the exercises would elevate my spirituality and enhance my sexuality."

125

Kate gathered that Dallas hadn't heard about Mary Frances's perpetual state of virginity.

"Totally disgusting, Kate. The second chink in Swami Schwartz's honor."

"When did Dallas tell you about the workshops?"

"Last night at Mancini's. In the ladies' room."

"When?" Kate sensed the timing was important. She couldn't recall Dallas and Mary Frances going off to the loo together.

"Shortly before Swami collapsed. I'd been dancing with Jack Gallagher, we came back to the table, then I went to the ladies' room. I think you were still dancing with Swami."

It had been on the dance floor with Swami stepping all over her new shoes that Kate had spotted Sanjay and Tiffani together at the bar, and Dallas Dalton heading out the front door. Laurence McFee had been dancing with his grandmother. And Mary Frances had been dancing with Jack. When the doctor had returned to the table, he'd asked where Dallas had gone and Sanjay, back from the bar, had answered, "Ladies' room." Maybe Sanjay believed that. Maybe not. Hadn't Mary Frances been at the table then? Kate thought so, but couldn't swear to it. Dallas had returned a few minutes later via the back door, located near the ladies' room and, maybe, she'd stopped there for a very brief visit. Yet . . . Dallas had left her Chanel clutch on the table. Would she have gone to the ladies' room without it?

As the sun bathed her in the last of its golden rays, Mary Frances appeared to have a halo.

Had Dallas used the ladies' room to try and conceal that walk around the block right before Swami's death? And, as part of her cover up, engaged Mary Frances in a topic that she wouldn't forget?

Or had the ex-nun lied? And, if so, why?

Twenty-one

The pier was alive with the sound of music. Tourists, local teenagers, condo retirees, and young couples with toddlers in tow listened to the steel drum's beat. A young man, wearing dreadlocks and a purple flowered silk shirt, sang, "Daylight come and I wanna go home." The festive mood proved contagious, taking Kate's mind off murder. Well, who said she and Marlene couldn't combine business with pleasure?

"The souvenir shops are doing great, aren't they?" Marlene pointed to a group of Canadian women all carrying shopping bags.

"There may be no room at the Inn."

"If not, we'll sit at the bar while we're waiting for a table, and you can buy me that martini. They're two for one during Happy Hour." To Kate's relief, Marlene had bounced back from her traumatic day.

"Fine, I want to ask Herb Wagner to recommend an attorney for Tiffani anyway."

The Neptune Inn had been a Palmetto Beach landmark for over forty years. With a front entrance off the pier and a side entrance off the sand, its two main attractions were the spectacular view of the Atlantic Ocean and the best fried shrimp, French fries, and cole slaw plate in South Florida.

Only a few months ago the pier, along with the restaurant and all the shops, had been about to be razed. Kate and Marlene, whose efforts helped keep the status quo, were glad to see Herb's Saturday night business booming.

"Ladies, welcome!" The deep voice came from a great bear of a man, around six-six and almost three hundred pounds. Herb Wagner hugged Marlene first, then Kate, who always worried during these greetings that he'd crack her ribs, then led them to the far end of the bar near the patio dining room. On cue, two young local guys, in shorts and polo shirts, jumped up, and offered them their seats.

"Thanks, boys," Herb said, then turned to Kate. "What are you gals drinking? It's on me."

"A martini, three olives, light on the vermouth, shaken not stirred." The twinkle was back in Marlene's eye.

Kate laughed. "When you've taken care of James Bond, I'll have a glass of white wine."

129

Ensconced on her bar stool, Marlene seemed totally relaxed in what she often referred to as her natural habitat.

As Kate was deciding whether to go over the suspects and their motives now or wait until they were seated at a table, Marlene's expression changed. "Here comes trouble."

Kate spun around to see Dallas Dalton, in skintight jeans and a spangled denim jacket, racing toward them.

"Sugar," she said, "I've been tracking you and Madam President down. Miss Mitford tipped me off that you'd be here."

"Your table is ready." Herb Wagner said, staring at Dallas.

"Could you make that a table for three, sugar?" Dallas's smile dazzled.

Herb, seemingly struck speechless, nodded.

"Well, lead the way, big boy. We gals have some serious business to discuss."

If Kate weren't so eager to question Dallas Dalton, she'd have resented and rejected the Texan's party crashing. For the second time in one day, Dallas had invited herself to Kate's table.

Once seated on the screened-in patio at a table inches from the sand, where they could hear the now-dark ocean's waves breaking, Dallas ordered another round of drinks, and a Cosmopolitan for herself. "Everything's on me, ladies, so eat large."

"What do you want, Dallas?" Marlene had kept quiet so far, but her testy tone bothered Kate. She didn't want Dallas leaving in a huff before she had some answers.

"Well, I'll tell you what I *don't* want, Marlene." Dallas sounded almost sincere. "I don't want you worrying your pretty little head about my condo or about the problems we may encounter with the building inspectors or any other agency. Just remember, there isn't anything that we can't fix. I promise you that. No matter how many changes are required. No matter how much those changes will cost."

Kate kicked Marlene's leg, urging her to remain silent.

"My dearly beloved late husband Shane left me a silo filled with money. More than enough money to make sure that I'd never have to deal with devilment again. And aren't government employees agents of Satan? No matter what they require us to repair, their demands, however unreasonable, will be met. And in addition, I plan on making a donation to the board, a most generous gift, to make Ocean Vista an even

131

more wonderful place to live."

Herb placed the drinks on the table, but apparently realizing they were engaged in Dallas's "serious business," only smiled and left.

In one swallow, Dallas downed almost half her Cosmopolitan. "I do want to fess up that I have one other teeny concern that we need to address."

The *need* word again. Dallas wanted something.

"What's that?" Marlene asked.

"I actually moved to Palmetto Beach because of Thistle. Shane's horse. Thistle was more famous than Trigger. And a better actor, I might add."

Kate giggled into her wine glass. Marlene didn't bother to cover up her laughter.

Dallas plowed on. "Thistle may — now mind you, just may — have to move in with me."

"You want to move a dead horse into Ocean Vista?" Marlene's voice carried, causing several diners to turn and stare at them with blatant curiosity.

Fascinated, but fearing fireworks, Kate said, "Well, I'm sure Thistle must be stuffed or . . ." Realizing she had no idea what she was talking about, she shut up.

What did taxidermists do anyway? And how were those amazingly lifelike bears, tigers, elephants, and even whales in New York City's Museum of Natural History preserved?

"Oh, you don't have to worry about that, I assure you Thistle's body is perfectly preserved."

Seeing the fury on Marlene's face, Kate tried again, "But Dallas, how would you get the horse into the condo?" She vividly recalled a baby grand piano being hoisted up twelve floors on a crane, then being pulled through a picture window into her cousin's co-op in Manhattan.

"The logistics do present a challenge," Dallas said, in that same calm, seemingly sincere, voice. She'd even toned down her twang. Could she do that on command? "I was thinking we might cut a hole in the roof."

Marlene drained her martini. "You're insane." She sounded almost as sincere as Dallas.

"Now, sugar," the twang made a comeback. "I said I'd pay for everything. Thistle is priceless. I'll up my donation to the Ocean Vista Board to a cool million. Hell, I'll buy the building."

Marlene sputtered, "You can't bribe me."

Dallas stood, reached into her denim jacket's pocket, and placed a hundred dollar bill on the table. "You're sweating, Marlene. No need to lose your cool. I only wanted to plant a seed. Thistle's original quarters may work out just fine." She winked at Herb Wagner who'd arrived with the menus. "Now you all will have to excuse me. Enjoy your dinner. I have a private yoga session scheduled with Sanjay Patel."

Twenty-two

Marlene ordered the lobster, flown in fresh from Maine. "Dallas Dalton has just replaced Mary Frances as my first choice for killer." She scanned the appetizers. "And, Herb, I'll start with a double shrimp cocktail."

"You don't really believe that Texas gal murdered Swami Schwartz, do you?" Herb, a wise man, asked in his pleasant, easygoing manner.

Kate savored the irony. Marlene's dislike of Dallas wouldn't stop her from using the hundred dollar bill to pay for dinner.

"No. And I don't think Mary Frances did, either." Marlene smiled. "But, wouldn't it be fun if one of those thorns in my tush turned out to guilty."

"Kate, what are you having?"

"My usual, Herb, the fried shrimp platter."

"It's on our nutty neighbor," Marlene said. "Have the lobster."

Kate gave her a dirty look. "I'm having the shrimp, Herb. And coffee. I have plans for after dinner and I've already had two glasses of wine."

Herb nodded and walked away.

"Plans?" Marlene had a two martini edge to her voice. "Are you driving somewhere?"

"Pass the rolls, please." Kate sounded pretty testy, herself.

While she wanted to discuss the suspects with Marlene, and looked forward to enjoying her favorite meal, Kate couldn't stop thinking about Life Preserver. Something she'd read in the company's prospectus. And something Dallas had said. Some sort of a link. Yes, definitely a link, albeit missing at the moment.

"No, I'm not going anywhere. I want to reread that file I downloaded this morning. If I have another drink, I'll fall asleep. It's been a long day, Marlene."

"Tell me about Tiffani. She's stopping by tonight, right? Any chance she slipped the cyanide into Swami's coffee?"

"Anything's possible, I suppose, but she did lead me to the computer files and she revealed a lot of secrets."

"Secrets that might be motives for several of the other suspects?"

"Well, yes."

"So maybe Tiffani's a lot smarter than

we think." Marlene's double shrimp cocktail had arrived. "Thanks, Herb, they look marvelous." Grabbing one by the tail, she whirled it around in the red sauce, then waved it in Kate's direction. "Can I tempt you?"

"I ordered the fried shrimp for dinner."

"Oh, hell, Kate, live dangerously. Try one of these, too."

Kate reached for the dripping shrimp, then laughed. "Who says I can't be flexible?"

"Anyone and everyone who has ever known you. But, tonight, with you wildly devouring two kinds of shrimp, I'm proud to say, you've proven them all wrong."

"Here's how flexible I can be: I'll accept any one of the suspects as our killer, though at the moment I'm leaning toward Danny Mancini."

"Really? I don't like to say this, but I think the sexy Sanjay, much as you admire him, is our guy." Marlene took a sip of her martini. "He's positively crawling with motives. He had the hots for Tiffani — even chatted her up at the bar on the night of the murder — and Swami's death certainly eliminated his competition, right? And, as a bonus, Sanjay wound up as director of the Yoga Institute. I wonder if he'd known he'd be stepping into Swami's position. And you told me how quickly he'd confirmed Tiffani's account of the scene between Laurence McFee and Swami. Could Sanjay have been trying to make Laurence appear guilty?" Marlene ate the last olive in her glass.

Had that been her third? Stop counting, Kate. She'd counted Charlie's beers when they'd been dating, trying to establish three as his limit. He hadn't been any easier to control than Marlene.

"Or, maybe, Sanjay's so smitten that he seconded Tiffani's story about them to keep me from focusing on her." It pained Kate to utter those words. She didn't want Tiffani to be guilty, didn't believe the girl could be capable of murder. Still . . . she couldn't be absolutely sure.

Marlene nodded. "And what about the charming Dr. Gallagher? He now owns the Yoga Institute outright."

"Yes, but he's such a wealthy man, owning the Institute doesn't strike me as a motive for murder." Once again the Life Preserver file floated through Kate's brain. Could that mysterious company, employing the likes of Harry Archer, be connected to Swami's death?

"With all these intriguing scenarios, why,

exactly, is Danny Mancini your prime suspect?"

Kate forced herself to focus; she'd deal with the file later. "Motive. Two, in fact. First motive: Revenge. According to Dallas, Swami refused Danny's request for a loan he desperately needed. Second motive: Greed. Swami put his godfather in his will. So now Danny has mucho money to pay off all his debts."

"Consider your source. I wouldn't believe anything that Texas twit said. And, for heaven's sake, Kate, who'd murder his own godson? Danny Mancini always struck me as a decent sort of guy."

"Another martini, Marlene?" Herb seemed to have a barkeep's unique radar, always appearing promptly when a customer ran out of fuel.

"Guess not, Herb." Marlene sounded resigned. "Kate and I have detective work to do tonight."

"Yeah, I overheard you two talking about the case. About that cute little blonde, Tiffani Cruz, and the handsome, young Indian doctor. About Danny." Kate sensed Herb Wagner had important information but wasn't quite sure if he wanted to share it.

"Is there something you'd like to tell us,

139

Herb?" Marlene had picked up the same vibe.

"Well, Tiffani used to wait tables here before she went to work at Ocean Vista. Occasionally, when I'm having my morning coffee, sitting out here on the patio, reading my newspaper, I see her and that young doctor exercising out on the beach, contorted into the strangest positions."

"Yoga," Kate said, feeling a pang of . . . what? Jealousy? Of a girl young enough to be her granddaughter? Resentment? Of her favorite instructor practicing yoga with another student? Had she totally lost her mind?

"Any fool could see that the guy was crazy about her, but Tiffani told my wife that she'd fallen madly in love with Swami Schwartz. Go figure. That young doctor's in trouble; Tiffani's a tease."

Kate wondered if Herb spoke from personal experience.

"What about Danny?" Marlene asked, her tenacity coming through loud and clear.

Herb sighed. "Look, I like Danny Mancini and I don't believe for a New York nanosecond that he killed Swami Schwartz. They were family, you know. But

140

that Dallas gal is right. Danny's a big gambler. Owes the mob more than a quarter of a million. He's not only in danger of losing the restaurant, he's in danger of losing his life." Herb wiped his beefy hand across his brow. "Or he was. Now, with this inheritance, he'll be okay again. At least, until the next sure thing. The next safe bet. Danny's addicted. He belongs in Gamblers Anonymous."

From some deep, dank recess of Kate's mind, Tiffani's tale about Detective Carbone and Danny Mancini going off together this morning, leaving the waitress and the young cop behind to pack up the evidence boxes, suddenly surfaced covered in muddy questions itching to be answered.

"Herb, do you know if Danny Mancini and Detective Carbone are friends? Maybe even longtime friends, from decades ago in New York?"

Herb's hound-dog jowls drooped to what she suspected might be an all-time low. "You're one sharp cookie, Kate Kennedy. Danny Mancini is Nick Carbone's godfather, too."

Twenty-three

If dessert hadn't been included in the price of her dinner, Kate would have gone straight home. But had she left after Herb's bombshell, she'd have forgotten to ask him to recommend an attorney for Tiffani. So now she and Marlene were wading through deepdish apple pie, topped with vanilla ice cream, and mulling over likely lawyers.

"Why don't we just put the three names in a hat and let Tiffani pick the winner?" Marlene asked, around a mouthful of pie. "I'm much more interested in Detective Carbone's relationship to Danny Mancini."

"Do you suppose many people know about that?" Kate somehow didn't think so.

"Let's see what we have here. Herb learned Danny was Nick Carbone's godfather during a poker game with Herb and Danny and two waiters from Mancini's. And you were right, Kate. Danny, Nick, and Swami had come from the same neighborhood."

"Most of those waiters have been at Mancini's since the sixties. Danny would have trusted them. Or maybe Danny didn't care if people knew Nick was his godson. Maybe it wasn't a secret." Kate sipped her coffee. "But Herb sure acted as if it were, and neither Mancini nor Carbone has ever mentioned it."

Marlene put her spoon down. "I'm outta here. Come on, Kate, let's go home. We have work to do."

A breeze had kicked up and the temperature had dropped some, but the crowd on the pier remained thick. Mostly teenagers starting out on this cool February evening, while the early-bird diners and the families with young children headed home.

Not wanting sand in their shoes, they walked back as they had come, along A1A, accompanied by the scent of hibiscus and the rustle of palm trees.

Almost no one walked anywhere in South Florida; tonight was no exception. In both the north and south lanes, traffic whizzed by. Saturday night drivers were always in a hurry. The Neptune Boulevard Bridge must be down, allowing quick access to the mainland. People going over to the movies on Federal Highway, or down to a café on Las Olas, or, maybe, out west to the track to bet on the trotters.

Charlie had loved the track. But Kate usually held the winning tickets. And the horses in the race, the jockey's record, the owners' colors had nothing to do with her success. She'd played the same Daily Double combination that her father had played for over forty years. Number Four to Win and Number Six to Show in the first race of the Daily Double; then Number Six to Win and Number Four to Show in the second race. Her father's betting logic: Number Four — for the number of letters in his first name: Bill. And Number Six — for the number of letters in his last name: Norton. Bill Norton had seldom lost. Nor had his daughter. Kate's winning "system" drove Charlie crazy. She smiled, remembering. The smile brought tears to her eyes. Even happy memories hurt.

"Godfather or not, Nick Carbone's too self-righteous to help Danny Mancini cover up a murder, don't you think?" Had Marlene spotted her tears and tried to distract her? No matter. As tired and vulnerable as Kate felt, it was better to have murder than memories on her mind.

"I'd like to think so, but this morning

144

godson and godfather took off together, leaving the crime scene evidence in the hands of Tiffani and a rookie cop. That's very strange behavior for such a by-the-book detective."

"Slow down, Kate." Marlene was panting. "That entire dinner seems to have settled in my esophagus."

Kate, who'd taken a Pepcid AC as a precaution before dinner, reached in her pocket and handed one to Marlene.

"I can't swallow this without water."

Tempted to say, then suffer, Kate nodded encouragingly. "Try. And, if you really can't get it down, we're only steps from the lobby. You can use the water fountain near the pool."

Marlene popped the tiny tablet into her mouth, then, looking miserable, shook her head. Moving slowly wouldn't help her sister-in-law's heartburn. Kate picked up the pace.

Amazing. At eight forty-five on a Saturday night, Ocean Vista's lobby was as deserted as a graveyard. Miss Mitford's desk area had gone dark and the piped-in music had been turned off. The water gurgling in Aphrodite's fountain seemed eerily loud in the silence.

Marlene, who'd kept her mouth shut until she'd reached the water fountain, had swallowed the tablet and was talking again.

"Spooky, isn't it? There must be a few live ones left in the dining room. What time does Tiffani finish up?"

"Nine-thirty." Kate pressed the elevator's up button.

"Hold that elevator, sugar."

Kate, recognizing the twang, turned around. Gone were the too-tight jeans and spangled denim jacket. Dallas now wore black yoga pants and a black cashmere sweatshirt. What she was carrying caught Kate's attention: A whip, crafted from rich cordovan leather.

"Well, ladies, I didn't reckon to run into you two so soon." Dallas glanced around the lobby. "Makes Death Valley look lively, don't it?"

"Are you bringing that whip up to your apartment?" Marlene sounded shrill, not unlike chalk scratching a blackboard.

"Sure am. Thistle's on his way home to mama."

"As president of Ocean Vista," the shrill had become a shriek, "I forbid you to bring that horse here. Your condo documents clearly state that we don't permit animals over twenty pounds."

146

If that were true, Kate had better put Ballou on a diet.

"Chill out, sugar. My original arrangements worked out. Thistle's moving into his new quarters on Monday. And tomorrow being Sunday, all the workmen are off, so tonight I'm going to sleep in my new home for the first time. Kind of a test run. I just brought this over from the hotel. Reminds me of Shane's and my days on the range." Dallas ran her hand over the leather on the whip, almost caressing it. "I never sleep without Thistle's saddle next to my bed."

They rode up to the third floor in dead silence.

"I could seriously strangle that woman," Marlene said, as they entered Kate's apartment, Ballou's yelps of joy and affectionate ankle nips greeting them.

Kate laughed. "One murder at a time, please."

Marlene scooped Ballou up and sat on Kate's off-white couch, holding the Westie in her lap.

"Well, I think I'm going to live. Your pill worked. I can breathe again. I'm going on a diet tomorrow."

"You're going up to Boca Raton tomorrow. Why put yourself in the path of

147

temptation? I'm sure the Lazarus Society will serve sustenance after the movie." Kate crossed the room and retrieved the Life Preserver prospectus from the top drawer of a desk near the door to the balcony. "Never start a diet on a Sunday."

"Is that like one of the ten commandments?"

"Yes. Number three." Kate sat down next to Marlene. Ballou sighed, obviously delighted to be in such close company with the two women he loved best.

"Does he have to go out again?" Marlene asked.

"No, he'd be sleeping if you weren't here spoiling him."

"Okay, hand me the prospectus."

While Marlene read aloud, Kate's mind wandered.

Funny how random ideas — seemingly unconnected — often waltzed together through her subconscious. Maybe talking about Marlene's viewing of *Death Takes a Holiday* set her strange but orderly dance sequence into motion: An image of a company up in Palm Beach that had been shut down by the city council segued to the funeral of a famous football player, then to the dead football star scoring a touchdown in Dallas Dalton's huge freezer, as a "perfectly preserved" Thistle cheered.

"Oh, my God!" Kate heard her voice crack.

"What's wrong?" Marlene jumped.

The doorbell rang.

Flustered and a little frightened at where her subconscious dance had led her, Kate went to let Tiffani in.

"I can't stay, Mrs. Kennedy," Tiffani said, by way of greeting. Then she actually blushed. "I have plans to meet Sanjay." She nodded at Marlene, "Hi, Ms. Friedman."

"I gather you're feeling better, Tiffani." Kate sounded almost as miffed as she felt. And didn't Sanjay Patel get around? Private yoga lessons with Dallas Dalton at six-thirty. Now a date with Tiffani Cruz. Reaching into her pocket, Kate pulled out the slip of paper Herb Wagner had given her. "There are three names here. Since Mr. Wagner has assured me these are the best attorneys in Broward County, Marlene and I were going to suggest drawing one of the three out of a hat."

Tiffani put the piece of paper in her pocket. Not an easy task. Her jeans were so tight, she could barely slide it in. "Thanks, Mrs. Kennedy, though I might not be needing any of them. Sanjay's kind of like

149

advising me. And he knows a really good lawyer."

She gave a little wave, pirouetted, and was out the door before Kate could think of a reply.

"Still think Tiffani's innocent?"

Kate said, "Annoying, yes. Guilty, no." Her mind was on the file in Marlene's hand.

"I can't say I understood most of this." Marlene held up the four-page prospectus. "Harry didn't seem bright enough to be part of such sophisticated research. What's all this scientific stuff about perfectly preserved patients?"

"Cryonics."

"I've heard that word before, but can't recall what it means. "Cry . . . on . . . ics." She enunciated as if she were in a spelling bee. "So what does Life Preserver actually do?"

"Freeze dead people."

Twenty-four

Kate might need post-life support herself if she couldn't calm down.

"Marlene, do you remember a company — I think it was called New Horizons — that opened up in Rico Mar, near Boca Raton, last year?" Sounding as if she were on speed, Kate didn't wait for an answer. "Some sort of a life extension lab that froze dead people and then, sometime in the future when medical science found the cure for whatever had killed them, would defrost the patients and bring them back to life. Perfectly preserved. Perfectly healthy. But the town, or maybe Palm Beach County, decided that the lab had violated some zoning or planning regulations and shut it down. I wonder who owned New Horizons? Not Dr. Gallagher — I'd remember that. Unless he'd been a silent partner. God! Could Jack Gallagher just have changed the company's name to Life Preserver and moved his cryonics business to Palmetto Beach?"

"Whoa! That's a real stretch, Kate."

"No stretch. Both Life Preserver and New Horizons offered buyers an afterlife that just keeps on going . . . like the Energizer bunny. Physical immortality with, as Harry Archer indicated, a spiritual twist. And that spiritual twist would be the Lazarus Society." Kate shook her head. "I wonder where your soul goes while your body's on ice?"

"Scary thought. But how can you be so sure you're right about Life Preserver being involved with cryonics?"

Sure? She'd stake her life on it. "Please, Marlene, listen to me. You need to get Harry Archer alone tomorrow after the screening and chat him up." Kate had deliberately used the *need* word. "Tell him you're sick and that when you die you don't want to be buried, you want your body to be frozen. Ask him if he has a price list."

Images of dead bodies suspended in an icy cold room, too awful to absorb and too intriguing to delete, floated through Kate's head, tormenting yet fascinating her.

"And for all these years, everyone has believed I'm the wild and crazy one."

Ballou got restless and struggled to jump off Marlene's lap. Could he be rebutting her sister-in-law's sarcastic tone?

Kate bent down to pet the Westie, stroking his soft white fur as he licked her hand. Not unlike one-upmanship during their childhood squabbles. Feeling foolish, she stood up.

"Marlene, maybe I really am crazy, but indulge me."

"Well, since you've indulged my schemes for sixty years, I guess it's my turn." As in the past, Marlene's warm smile brightened Kate's mood. "You do realize that Swami Schwartz, as Gallagher's partner, must have known and supported Life Preserver's goals."

Kate nodded. "No doubt Swami planned on being one of those 'perfectly preserved patients' who'd be frozen after death, then brought back to life. What he hadn't planned on was being murdered. Or having an autopsy."

"Yeah. I'll bet a cryonics patient can't be embalmed, never mind whatever gross stuff a coroner does during a post-mortem."

A wave of sadness swept over Kate and in its wake, mercifully, carried away the images of dead bodies from her mind. Suddenly, she felt angry and more deter-mined than ever to find Swami's killer.

"You know, Kate, if Tiffani told the

truth about the screaming match between Laurence McFee and Swami Schwartz, then Magnolia's grandson might well be our prime suspect. According to Tiffani, Laurence said he'd see Swami dead before he'd allow the McFee money to be used for some science fiction project. Talk about frozen assets."

"Talk about a bad pun." Kate felt better. Marlene seemed to be buying into her theory. "And Sanjay seconded Tiffani's report. I'll spend some time with Laurence McFee at the memorial rehearsal tomorrow night."

"Who ever heard of a rehearsal for a funeral? Fitzgerald was right. 'The very rich are different from you and me.' " Marlene shook her head.

As wound up as she was, Kate grinned, then went right back to the suspects. "Last night at Mancini's, Dallas Dalton was questioning Jack Gallagher about the Lazarus Society as I approached the table. He never answered her." Kate closed her eyes trying to conjure up the scene. "Then later when Magnolia McFee arrived, she wanted to know if Dallas had joined the Lazarus Society, actually saying, 'We need fresh blood.' But Dr. Gallagher immediately blocked my view of Dallas, so I couldn't hear her response." Kate shuddered. "While Magnolia's remark didn't seem suspicious then, now I'm convinced the Lazarus Society must be some kind of support group for Life Preserver."

"If you're right, Kate, I promise I'll find out the truth tomorrow. I'll wheedle it out of Handsome Harry."

"If I'm right, you won't have to drag it out of him. Harry Archer's a salesman; just let him know you want to live forever. Your date-to-die-for will be delighted to reserve you a spot in cold storage."

"Speaking of cold, what about Dallas Dalton's freezer?" Marlene squinted, her well-arched brows narrowing. "Could it be her very own cryonics alternative to Life Preserver? A really chilly stable for her beloved Thistle? Maybe that horse isn't stuffed. Maybe he's frozen."

Kate laughed aloud. It felt good. "Marlene, you've just raced ahead of me!"

At eleven-thirty, an hour after Marlene had gone home, Kate, totally exhausted, was still at the computer. "This has been the longest day of my life, Charlie." She'd been having one-sided conversations with her husband ever since he'd dropped dead at their condo closing nine months ago.

Her anger had abated, but her sense of loss lingered.

She so missed this man. Her lover and her friend. A man's man who listened like a woman and never seemed to judge. "Would you ever have considered being frozen?" God, could she be feeling guilty about not having provided Charlie Kennedy with a chance to come back? Or was she just brain dead?

Now, after researching on the Web, knowing more about cryonics than any nonbeliever would want to learn, Kate held her head.

Some cryonics companies offered extensive premedication, some didn't feel that was necessary for a successful suspension. Most claimed to preserve brain and body structure from decay by cooling the "patient" as rapidly as possible and using cryoprotectants to reduce freezing damage.

Freezer burn seemed to be a real concern, but the correct neurovitrification process, injection with anticoagulants prior to washout — Kate groaned — and perfusion with glycerol should eliminate that problem.

Patients who wanted to preplan had two options: Full body suspension. Or head only. The proponents of the latter believed that bringing back your brain would do the trick of regenerating the body.

One website boasted about the company's low cost. Though prices could soar to over $120,000, a real bargain — for a head only — was offered at $29,000. But Kate couldn't determine if that included transportation. Some labs only prepared cryogenics patients who would then be transported to a storage facility where they'd be suspended in canisters filled with liquid nitrogen, and preserved at a temperature of minus 320 degrees.

Two companies provided both patient preparation and storage. One had a "Family Plan." Moving from site to site seemed like a trip through the *Twilight Zone*.

How she and Charlie had loved that show.

Kate sighed, turned off her computer, and went to bed alone.

Twenty-five

The sun broke through the horizon as a golden halo of light, then settled into the sky like a huge tangerine, warming her yoga mat on the sand as Kate eased into the Upside Down Dog. At her side, Ballou mimicked her movement, kicking some sand in the process. The Westie appeared to have mastered the position far better than she. Kate's laughter interrupted any chance that she might actually achieve a state of meditation. Her mind, in full throttle since a nightmare about floating heads had jarred her awake at six, showed no signs of slowing down.

She savored the solitude of the empty beach. Sitting with her legs crossed yogi style, breathing in the fresh air, she stared out at the waves cresting in the ocean, then crashing against the shore, glad that she had worn her zip-up nylon jacket in this cool breeze, glad to be alive. Even without Charlie? She bit her lip. Damn, the answer was yes.

Slowly she stood and stretched, linking her hands behind her back, then touching her toes with ease. Her knees didn't crack as they had when she started yoga lessons less than three months ago. For a woman of a certain age, she'd mastered the basics quickly. Her balance and her strength had both improved. So had her shape. Tummy tighter. Arms slightly — ever so slightly — firmer. Back straighter. And, even with less than six hours sleep — though she'd have preferred eight — she felt good.

A tall, lean young woman, the one she'd seen on the beach before, with two small boys in tow, walked south from the pier.

Kate's memories of her early years — triggered by a smell, a glimpse, or an overheard word — would unfold like a movie, starring herself as a little girl with long, chestnut curls wearing a brown jumper and a beige linen blouse with puffed sleeves. Truly hideous, even in memory. "I hate my uniform, Mommy." A line of dialogue added authenticity. And she saw action: Walking to school, sitting in a classroom filled with girls — she'd never been in a class with boys — reading a history assignment. Those early memories were so fast-paced, they played more like coming attractions than movies. Fragments from an era long gone, but held dear.

Some memories remained silent. Still

shots. Black and white photographs. Period pieces, frozen in time. Her grandmother's firm jaw and kind eyes. Her mother and father dressed up for a party. Mommy pretty in a frilly, forties' hat. Daddy handsome in a dark suit and tie. Both so young.

Other memories were felt rather than seen. Out of the past, often unbidden, a memory became a moment, an emotion that intruded on the present. A preteen girl embarrassed by her skinny legs. Or a young mother overwhelmed by the responsibility of caring for two toddlers who could both outrun and outfox her.

Forty years ago, Kate had been the young woman passing by. This morning, she ached to reach out and touch the little boys.

Memory could suck you in and not let you escape. In the days following Charlie's death, Kate had wallowed in that abyss. Remembering the dead had become her life.

Ballou whined, then nipped at her ankle.

"Okay, let's take that walk." Trying to get a leash on an excited, yapping, jumping Westie brought Kate back to the business at hand.

She felt a twinge of excitement herself,

wanting to get started on her day. So much to do. Right after the walk, she'd go to church. Life might be moving on, but she could take the time to stop and light a candle for Charlie.

Ballou led the way, north toward the pier. While Kate had been down memory lane, several more people had established a beachhead. Two young men, heading south, waved as they jogged by.

She picked up a piece of driftwood, slender and bleached by seawater and sunshine to an ash gray, considering, than rejecting bringing it up to the apartment.

Near the pier two slender forms, one with flaxen hair, one with hair black as coal, stood side by side, stretching their palms toward the sky. Tiffani and Sanjay starting their morning with yoga on the beach, just as Herb Wagner had reported.

If only she could eavesdrop. But Palmetto Beach's wide expanse of white sand offered nowhere to hide. They were still several yards away and, seemingly, totally absorbed. Should she approach them? Say good morning?

While debating, she heard a man's voice call out. "Is that you, Kate Kennedy?"

She pivoted to the right. Danny Mancini, dressed as if ready to play host at his restaurant, in a white shirt and tie, lightweight gray wool trousers, and with sand spilling out of his black leather loafers, barreled down on her.

She staggered, backing away toward the ocean. What the devil was Danny doing here? Ballou barked. Not warmly. Kate must have conveyed her fear.

"Sorry, I didn't mean to startle you."

In the bright sunlight, he looked haggard. And his words sounded slurred. Could the man be drunk at seven-thirty in the morning? She hesitated, then took a step forward. Danny didn't seem dangerous. Just confused, out of it.

"Are you okay?"

"Yes." He held his head. "No. I'm feeling sick, Kate." Though the breeze remained cool, sweat ran down Danny's face.

She touched his arm. Under the damp shirt, his entire body was shaking. So was Kate.

"Come with me, back to Ocean Vista. I'll call nine-one-one." Damn! Why wasn't she carrying the cell phone Marlene had given her?

"Mr. Mancini, do you need help?" Tiffani Cruz, too, was covered in sweat, but on her, it glowed, like a beacon highlighting youth and good health. She

162

whipped out a phone, no bigger than a matchbook, from an invisible pocket in her black spandex pants.

Sanjay Patel arrived right behind her, and spread a large beach towel on the sand. "Please lie down, Mr. Mancini." Sanjay helped Danny lower himself onto the towel, held a finger to Danny's neck, then turned to Tiffani. "Ask nine-one-one to dispatch an ambulance. Tell them to come immediately."

"But . . ." Tiffani's voice broke.

"Dial it now!" The doctor ordered.

Thank God! Sanjay had taken control. In her panic, Kate had completely forgotten that a doctor was exercising on the beach. Literally steps away.

As Sanjay loosened his tie, Danny whispered, "I'm a . . ."

"A what?" Sanjay asked, leaning in closer.

Danny moaned, then closed his eyes.

Twenty-six

St. Elizabeth's on A1A in Palmetto Beach, two blocks north of Ocean Vista, was a prime example of one of the major differences between New York City and South Florida: Architecture. With its light and airy modern design, its vaulted ceilings, white walls, and planked flooring, and the abstract art in its stained-glass windows, St. Elizabeth differed dramatically from the wonderful old, gothic-style churches that Kate had attended as a child, from her beloved St. Patrick's on Fifth Avenue . . . to St. Agnes Cathedral in Rockville Centre where she and Charlie had been parishioners and the boys had been baptized.

As the church bells tolled ten times, Kate knelt and prayed for Danny Mancini. She truly believed he'd be okay, but a little insurance couldn't hurt.

On the beach while they'd waited for nine-one-one to answer, Tiffani explained that Danny Mancini was a diabetic, then rummaged, in vain, through his pockets looking for insulin. But Sanjay had her run

164

over to the Neptune Inn to get some sugar or jam. When the nine-one-one operator got on the line, Sanjay quickly identified himself as a doctor and asked the operator to alert the paramedics that the patient was in shock.

By the time Danny had been whisked off to the Palmetto Beach Medical Center, both the paramedics and the doctor agreed the patient would make it. Kate felt grateful Tiffani and Sanjay had gone to the hospital with Danny. She couldn't go with Ballou in tow.

Could Danny Mancini have been ill yesterday morning when he and Nick Carbone took off from the restaurant with no explanation? At Dinah's, Tiffani hadn't mentioned an episode of any sort, not even giving a hint about Mancini having felt unwell. Indeed, she'd implied that he and Carbone had gone off together because of a phone call that the detective had received. Then this morning, when Kate asked her if Danny had been feeling ill yesterday, Tiffani had shrugged and said, "Maybe. He never felt really good, you know. But nothing like this. I'd have noticed if Mr. Mancini had been this sick."

As the organist played, "Let There Be Peace on Earth," and the congregation sang one of her favorite hymns, Kate wondered if Tiffani really hadn't noticed her boss's condition. Or had the girl outright lied?

Enough, Kate. She chided herself and joined in for the second verse.

After the mass ended, Kate lighted candles for Charlie, her parents, his parents, and for Kevin, Jennifer, Lauren, and Katharine, Peter and Edmund, for both of Marlene's dead husbands, and then feeling guilty, another for Marlene's only living ex-husband and, of course, for Swami Schwartz and Danny Mancini. The church suddenly seemed ablaze, every candle in the vigil tray in front of the altar flickering.

Kate wasn't especially religious, not even spiritual, as so many people professed to be these days. She pictured God as a Santa Claus figure, and she believed in an equal opportunity afterlife — maybe it would include some sort of telepathy so all souls could stay in touch, not unlike, but better than, her one-sided conversations with Charlie.

Well, her theory made more sense than Life Preserver freezing a "patient's" head and hoping that one day in the distant future, science could reignite his brain and let it grow a new body.

166

★ ★ ★

As luck would have it, the bridge was up, so she arrived at Einstein Bagels on Federal Highway a few minutes after eleven. She liked to come here on Sundays to start the *New York Times* crossword puzzle, enjoy a fresh cinnamon raisin bagel with cream cheese, and sip a cup of coffee. Life's simple pleasures. Kate was a tea drinker, but the coffee at Einstein's smelled and tasted so good, she couldn't resist.

She found a small table off in a corner, plopped her tray and newspaper down, and opened the magazine section.

"Good morning, Mrs. Kennedy."

Drat. She looked up, then smiled. She didn't mind being interrupted by Jeff Stein, the young New York City transplant, who edited the *Palmetto Beach Gazette*.

"Hi. Sit down, Jeff." He was balancing a tray holding coffee and an onion bagel.

With a little rearranging of newspapers, trays, and chairs, he sat.

"Looking good, Mrs. K." Jeff had actually seemed to assess her before giving the compliment. "And remember my job offer is still on the table." He pushed his plate to one side. "Well, it would be if there were any room on this table."

167

A job as a reporter. Kate rolled the word around. Food for the brain. As tasty as her cinnamon raisin with cream cheese. Granted, she'd mostly cover local news. Nothing very exciting. Bingo winners at the Senior Center. Sixtieth anniversaries. Condo meetings. And she'd write lots of obituaries. Still, she'd be a reporter. The idea tempted her.

"You haven't hired anyone yet?"

"No. And I can't run the *Gazette* all by myself, Mrs. K." He wiped cream cheese off his mouth. "Think about it, will you?"

She nodded. "I promise I'll let you know in a day or two."

"You were at that dinner party Friday night where Swami Schwartz was poisoned, right? Wouldn't you like to report on that? You know: Where, when, why, and whodunit."

"Well, that sounds better than writing his obituary."

"Dr. Jack Gallagher's taken care of that. I found Swami's obit on my desk first thing this morning. Almost as if the good doctor had written it in advance."

"Jeff, what do you know about Life Preserver?"

His thick black brows flew up in a pretty good imitation of Groucho Marx's leer.

"You never cease to amaze, Mrs. K. Life Preserver. Now that's a real mystery. Just how do *you* know about the best-guarded business secret in Palmetto Beach?"

Kate made a big thing out of slowly chewing her bagel. If she didn't talk, she figured Jeff's curiosity couldn't tolerate silence.

Jeff took a swig of coffee, then spoke in a low voice. "The mayor is up in arms. He and the town council may not understand most of Life Preserver's scientific jargon, but they know the company has something to do with cryonics research. Gallagher charmed the zoning board, seems to have them in his pocket, but with all those holy rollers on the town council, the doctor, despite a popularity bordering on sainthood, may have to take his business elsewhere."

Kate swallowed the last of her bagel and smiled. "Mind you, I have no proof, but it might not be the first time that Dr. Gallagher has moved his business."

Jeff stared at her, his mouth a perfect O and his bushy brows shot up again. "What do you mean?"

"New Horizons." Kate said, with far more confidence than she felt. "I suspect Dr. Gallagher funded that venture — as a silent partner — and when Rico Mar or

169

Palm Beach County shut the company down, Gallagher just changed its name to Life Preserver and moved his lab down to Palmetto Beach, where he believed the climate might be more friendly." She paused, then went for the kill. "And I don't believe Life Preserver only does cryonics research. I think Dr. Gallagher will be freezing dead bodies and then suspending his *patients* or, in some cases, just their heads in canisters until a cure for whatever killed them is found."

Jeff gulped. "If we break that story, Mrs. K, we'll be the Woodward and Bernstein of Palmetto Beach."

She meant to take a right off Federal Highway, cross the bridge, and head home. But her old car, acting as if it had a mind of its own, wound up in the left lane, so she drove west.

The entrance to the Palmetto Beach Industrial Park was east of I-95, just off Powerline Road, and three blocks north of Neptune Boulevard. Though located in a marginal area of town, the park itself was more upscale than she'd expected. Kate wondered how Tiffani's apartment could be nearby; this was definitely not a residential area.

★ ★ ★

Behind a chain-link fence — though the gate was open — and amid carefully tended shrubs and lots of green, there were maybe thirty businesses in small, medium, and large beige stucco buildings. Mostly wholesale warehouses: women's clothes, beauty supplies, an electrical outlet, a costume jewelry factory, a television repair center. All clearly marked. Large signs or billboards heralded the product or service. Since she had no address, she drove around four times before she noticed the tiny bronze plaque on one of the larger beige buildings that identified Life Preserver.

Midday on a Sunday, the park was eerily empty. No people. No cars. She stopped and stepped out to investigate. Nothing out of the ordinary about the warehouse. What was out of the ordinary was its steel door, barred windows, and enormous NO TRESPASSING sign. Not to mention the armed guard who'd just walked around from the back of the warehouse and was heading straight for her.

Twenty-seven

Jack Gallagher held Danny Mancini's hand, noting how mottled and veined his thin skin looked. "You'll be okay, you old fool. And you have only me to thank. Left to your own devices, you'd have been dead decades ago, with no hope of ever coming back." Jack hated waste and Danny had wasted his first time around, abusing his body, a temple to be revered, and now frittered away these last precious days in the autumn of his life with his compulsive gambling and destroyed his body with booze, tobacco and, though a long-diagnosed diabetic, a chocolate addict. Amazing he'd remained so slender. Jack had always thought that Danny resembled Tony Randall, one of his all-time favorite actors.

Danny moaned. Jack glanced at the monitor behind his bed. Vital signs were stable. The window in the posh private room on the top floor of the Palmetto Beach Medical Center faced southeast, offering an ocean view, but Danny's eyes remained closed. Jack suspected that his patient wasn't sleeping, but merely avoiding any conversation with his doctor. Since Jack felt more in the mood to lecture than chat, that worked for him.

"Swami left you a legacy, the best spot and the finest canister in Life Preserver's freezer. You'll be too far gone to preserve, no longer a candidate for vitrification, if you continue to live like a drunk and a glutton. I'm warning you, Danny, you'll be embalmed and put into the ground, covered with dirt. Buried. For God's sake, man, do you want to spend eternity in a grave? What's wrong with you?"

Jack felt disgust and anger, but also pity. Danny blinked, but remained silent, adding another sin to the doctor's list. "And your godson left you money. Lots of money. You'll have more than enough to pay off your debts. Wake up and live. Aren't things bad enough? This is all so inconvenient."

Danny opened his eyes. "So how much money are we talking about?"

In the yellow and white waiting room, Jack found Sanjay Patel and Tiffani Cruz — even her name made him shudder — sitting in two of the white wicker chairs. The cozy room, one of many decorated under Jack's guidance, reflected the Pal-

173

metto Beach Medical Center's image and reputation. Lovely immaculate surroundings, with an excellent caring staff providing the finest medical care in the best HMO in South Florida. Jack loved how the chairs' yellow and white striped cushions exactly matched the yellow walls.

But then he loved everything about the building, fussing over it like the child he'd never had: the art deco design, the state-of-the-art operating rooms, the well-equipped rehabilitation wing, the laboratories, like autoclaves, where all the patients' tests were done in-house, and even the cafeteria with, if not gourmet, more than acceptable food.

What he loved most of all was that the public rooms never smelled like a hospital, weren't constant reminders of sick patients. He'd banned the scent of ammonia from all the visitors' lounges.

"How is he?" Sanjay asked.

"Much improved." Jack pulled a wicker hassock up to Sanjay's chair and showed him Danny's chart.

Such a stunning young man. Jack couldn't wait for him to join the medical center's staff as soon as he passed the Florida Boards. And so suave. What a great Yoga Institute director he'd make. As

174

much as Jack had admired Swami, the yogi had never lost his brash Brooklyn attitude, making him difficult to work with. Jack had been totally against Swami's Tantra Workshop. Sex and spirituality, indeed. More like the old girls getting a cheap thrill.

"Can I see Mr. Mancini?" Tiffani stood up.

Impertinent little tramp, wasn't she? What could Sanjay, an educated, refined young man possibly see in her? Even Swami Schwartz had rejected her advances. And he hadn't been a man who'd said no easily.

"Sorry, Miss Cruz. He's sleeping. Maybe if you come back later." Jack spread his arms out in front of him. "Much later. This evening?" He hoped he didn't sound inviting.

"Gee, Dr. Gallagher, have you forgotten we all have a command performance up at Magnolia McFee's tonight? All us people who were at the table when Swami died."

He had forgotten. Or erased it from his memory. "So we do. Well, as I say, you can't see Mr. Mancini now."

Sanjay took her hand. "Come on, Tiffani, let's get you home."

Jack smiled. "Perhaps, you'd like to stop

back this afternoon, Sanjay. Danny asked to see you."

A bold-faced lie. But it worked. Sanjay nodded. "Please tell Mr. Mancini I'll be back later."

On his way back to reinforce Danny Mancini's reformation, Jack rehearsed his lines, much as tonight at Magnolia's they'd be rehearsing their readings and eulogies for Swami's memorial. That bloody woman always had to be in charge. Ordering everyone around at the Lazarus Society meetings. Deciding how her donations should be spent at the Yoga Institute. Demanding to check out his cryonics research. Well, damn that control freak. Jack had prepared his eulogy and wouldn't allow his words to be edited. And he'd tell Magnolia that tonight. He'd have to pass on *Death Takes a Holiday*, but he'd be damned if he'd miss the chance to speak to Harry Archer's prospects at the reception after the movie, so he might be a tad late for the rehearsal.

"If Danny continues drinking, smoking, and going on sugar sprees with a vengeance, he'd be better off dying right now, wouldn't he, Jack?" A grating twang spoke his thoughts aloud.

"Dallas, what the hell are you doing here?" Jack felt his blood pressure rapidly rising.

"Is that any way to greet a gal?" Dallas' throaty laugh filled the quiet corridor. "I spent my first night at Ocean Vista, had my coffee on my balcony, and watched the action on the beach. I knew that ambulance would bring Danny Mancini straight to you, Jack."

Don't let this brassy blonde get to you. Rhinestones in the morning. Jeans two sizes too small. Trailer trash who'd slept her way through Texas. Shane Dalton could have taken first prize in the state fair's cuckolded husband contest.

"You'll have to excuse me, Dallas, I have patients to see."

"As long as you have Thistle in your appointment book for tomorrow afternoon. I trust those steel workers have completed the sliding door into Life Preserver's cold storage area. They surely billed me for mucho money." Her red lipstick cracked in the corners of her mouth. Vile. But then, overhead fluorescent lighting was cruel. "Why do you keep staring at me, Jack? You *are* ready for Thistle's arrival, aren't you?"

"Look here, Dallas, the zoning board has approved the cryonics research, including animal testing in our lab, but the town council may want to do an on-site visit. How can I hide a horse?" God knows he had enough to hide. "Can't you wait a week?" He sounded desperate. "Why are you being so damn unreasonable?" Jack's voice broke. "Do you want to be responsible for Life Preserver being shut down?"

"I've given you more than enough time. And money." The twang turned sour. "You're long past the date we agreed on. So, listen up. Give the town council a tour in the morning. Or charm them out of ever taking a tour. Charm's your stock in trade, Jack. Either way, I've gone to great effort and expense arranging for Thistle to be wrapped in dry ice and transported from Arizona in a custom-designed refrigerated van. My horse is scheduled to arrive Monday at four. I expect you to be prepared to accommodate him."

Jack cheerfully could have killed her, and he'd make certain that she never had a cryonics chance to be brought back to life.

"Now, will you kindly direct me to Danny's room or do I have to go back to the information desk?" The twang sweetened. "We shouldn't be squabbling, Jack. Our work is too important. And besides, we're going to spend eternity together, aren't we?"

"The last door on the left, number four-o-one." He raised his chin. After all, he was in charge of his own medical center. "I'm going with you, Dallas. You can say hello, but that's all. Danny's too sick to have visitors."

In an uneasy truce, they arrived at the room, but Danny was nowhere to be found.

How could Danny Mancini have managed to put on his sandy clothes and just walk out of the hospital? No one, not the charge nurse, or the aide, or the orderly, or anyone at the fourth floor nursing station, or the reception desk had seen him leave.

Jack decided to stop by Danny's cottage on Cherry Blossom Lane, a few blocks west of Federal Highway, though he doubted he would find Danny at home. And he had his priorities. His first stop would be at the Palmetto Beach Industrial Park, to confirm that the workers had shown up today to complete their final test on the sliding door, making sure absolutely no hot air could penetrate its steel. Then he'd figure out a way to dissuade the town council from visiting. He felt a little better.

Dallas had been right about his charm. He'd invite the mayor to breakfast.

As he pulled up to Life Preserver, he spotted an old Chevy. An unlikely vehicle for the steel workers. Jack watched the guard coming around from the right side of the building, then picking up his pace and, suddenly, reaching for his revolver. Only then did Jack see the slim, silver-haired woman heading toward the front door. She looked familiar. Of course! Kate Kennedy. She'd been at the dinner party last night when Swami died. Came with Mary Frances, the dancing ex-nun. A widow, he thought. And, at Swami's recommendation, about to become the Yoga Institute's newest board member. What the hell was she doing here?

Twenty-eight

Kate felt like Mata Hari. Right before the firing squad executed her. Not only had the uniformed guard reached for his weapon, someone had slammed a car door behind her.

"Can't you read, lady?" The guard gestured with his gun to the NO TRESPASSING sign.

"Sorry." Kate floundered, frightened, listening to the footsteps behind her, and not knowing what to say.

"Mrs. Kennedy, isn't it?" That refined, silky smooth voice could only belong to Jack Gallagher. Great. Caught with her hand in his cryonics cookie jar. She spun around.

"Put that gun away," the doctor ordered. Then he smiled at Kate. "Please accept my apology. This is no way to treat a lady."

"It ain't my fault," the guard grumbled. "I'm no mind reader, Dr. Gallagher. How was I to know you and the intruder are friends?"

Excuses jumbled around in Kate's mind.

None made any sense. What in heaven's name could she say to Jack Gallagher? Help me, Charlie!

"What can I do for you, Mrs. Kennedy?"

Serious. Caring. Uncompromising. Kate had no doubt this was the same voice the doctor used when explaining to a patient that his illness was terminal. Probably med students were taught the right timbre, practiced just the right inflection. Then, unaccountably, she giggled, thinking his potential Life Preserver "patients" might not sweat a diagnosis of death.

"Are you feeling unwell, Mrs. Kennedy?"

Charlie had to have inspired her. Fear vanished, and she spoke boldly, "I couldn't feel better, thank you. I've heard about your cryonics research. And I'm most intrigued. Who wouldn't want the chance to come back from the dead? I'm writing an article for the *Palmetto Beach Gazette*." Jack Gallagher's shocked expression tickled her. "My editor, Jeff Stein, sent me." It wouldn't hurt for the doctor and the guard to believe that someone had known she was coming here. "Dr. Gallagher, could you take me on a tour of Life Perserver?"

On her way home, Kate credited Charlie

and all those blazing candles for her easy escape. Jack Gallagher had refused — most politely, very smoothly, and somewhat vaguely — her request for a tour, saying that he had to deal with some workmen today and the lab would remain off limits for visitors, even the press, until their job had been completed. Then he walked her to her car and told her he'd bring some information about his cryonics research to Magnolia McFee's tonight. Still, she'd come away with the distinct impression that the doctor didn't want any publicity for Life Preserver, not even a favorable newspaper article.

To think she'd been attracted to that smooth operator, even for a fleeting moment. Charlie must be chuckling.

With bright sunshine streaming through the car's open windows as she waited to cross the bridge, Kate felt, despite her sadness over the yogi's death, a sense of excitement. God, she loved a mystery.

One of seven people had murdered Swami Schwartz. Kate had eliminated Mary Frances as a suspect. A decision based on gut combined with faith. What Nick Carbone would dismiss as woman's intuition. As if she cared what he thought.

She had to prune the field. Tonight, she'd have a chance to observe all seven up close and personal at the McFee mansion. How Agatha Christie was that?

The suspects: Tiffani Cruz, Danny Mancini, Dallas Dalton, Jack Gallagher, Sanjay Patel, Laurence McFee, and his grandmother, Magnolia, all had the opportunity, and most of them seemed to have motives, as well. That left the means. Swami's murder had been premeditated. Which of the seven had carried cyanide to the dinner party to spike his coffee?

As she exited the bridge, the scent of freshly baked bread coming from Dinah's Restaurant wafted through the car windows. Kate inhaled. Delicious. Detective work required energy. She'd stop at Dinah's before heading home.

Ballou greeted her as if she'd been gone for days instead of hours. "Now be a good boy. If you stop yelping and nipping at my ankles, I'll share this rye bread with you." A very tiny piece.

He followed her into the kitchen and she put the kettle on for tea. While she easily could have devoured the loaf neat — while thinking, balanced diet, Kate — she rummaged in the refrigerator for a slice of cheese and a bit of tomato to create a sandwich.

Taking her lunch and her portable phone to the balcony, she marveled at how crowded the beach was. Colorful blankets staked out claims on patches of sand, chairs lined the shore, the surfers had multiplied threefold, and she wasn't eating alone. Half the sun bathers, glistening in oil or spotted with white lotion, were munching on hot dogs and fries. A few families had brought homemade sandwiches much like her own. High season — she'd better get used to it — snowbirds and tourists would be here till Easter.

Between bites, Kate checked her messages.

"This is Tiffani Mrs. Kennedy. Mr. Mancini's doing okay, I guess. Dr. Gallagher wouldn't let me see him. Sanjay's going back to the hospital this afternoon. But I need to tell you — uh — there's something odd — oh, never mind, I'll talk to you later."

Something odd? She'd give Tiffani a call.

"Kate, I'm getting ready for my date to die for — hell that's more eerie than funny now, right? Should I wear black? Give me a call."

Kate glanced at her watch. Not quite

185

one. She'd had such a full morning, it seemed much later than that. Maybe after she called Tiffani, she'd pop over to Marlene's and check out her outfit.

"Nana, this is Katharine. All's well here. Lauren made the Dean's list. Thank God, my GPA will never get me accepted into Harvard. Who'd want to follow in big sister's designer-shod footsteps? Dad's great. Never misses my soccer games. Sends his love. Mom's making money by the minute. She wants to take me to Paris for spring break . . . But I'd like to come stay with you, if that's okay. I need some sun and surf . . . and I miss you, Nana."

Katharine, her favorite girl. Her namesake. So like Charlie, boasting her grandfather's red hair, only now as she turned seventeen it was darkening to auburn. Freckles scattered across the bridge of her pug nose and kissed her cheeks. A fuller face and rounder body than her older sister, the tall, willowy blonde who favored Jennifer's family.

Kate sighed. Kevin's Lowell in-laws might be smarter, richer, and far more prominent, but the Kennedys were warmer, wittier, and far more fun. Especially Peter and his partner, Edmund. Kate would welcome Katharine with open arms, but convincing Jennifer that she and her daughter would *always have Paris* might be a hard sell.

Still . . . the words had worked for Rick Blaine. Ilsa Lund changed her travel plans. It was worth a try.

Twenty-nine

Since Tiffani wasn't home, Kate left a message. Katharine didn't answer her cell phone either, so she left another message. Nana-speak. A language between grandmother and granddaughter. "Yes, I'd love to have you here, but we'll have to get your mother to buy into it."

Was anyone ever there when you called back? Telephone tag. The great American game, replacing real tag, with the tap on the shoulder and the shout, "You're out!"

Kate put the dishes in the sink, then said, "Okay, Ballou, we're going to visit Auntie Marlene." The little dog cocked his head as if to say, "Really? You mean it?" Then he yipped and jumped in ecstasy — his vocabulary definitely included the word *Marlene*.

Her former sister-in-law's apartment looked better in dim light. Marlene always had been casual about housekeeping and would never willingly part with any possession, but now her stuff had taken over her space.

Located on Ocean Vista's first floor, with a balcony literally hanging over the sand, Marlene's condo had been beautifully and expensively furnished. With shoes, hats, purses, shopping bags, clothes, and a myriad of unidentifiable clutter strewn over every chair, sofa, and bed, Kate could only attest to those furnishings because she'd helped Marlene move in ten years ago. Ballou loved to visit, nuzzling the stray cashmere sweater or soft old sock on the floor, probably thinking of the apartment as one big playpen. And to complete his picture of heaven, Marlene came through with a Triscuit — her grudging concession to doggie health.

"It's about time." Marlene, wearing a pink silk dressing gown with marabou feathers that could have come straight from a forties' movie set, sounded breathless. "Come with me, I need help."

Glancing at her watch, Kate, with Ballou on her heels, followed Marlene into her bedroom. "When do you have to leave?"

"Five minutes ago. Hurry up!" She held up two dresses, one a Pucci print, mostly orange and yellow. The other a purple chiffon.

Kate shook her head and headed for the closet. "Where's your black Irish linen

189

dress that drapes so well?"

"I wasn't serious about wearing black, Kate. I only bought that dress in case I had to go to a funeral. At our age, one never knows. If I were going to Swami's memorial, I'd wear it."

Kate opened the closet door and all sorts of stuff tumbled off the top shelf and onto her head. Sixty years melted away. She was a kid again, listening to the old radio show, Fibber McGee and Molly. Fibber had the same problem with his hall closet.

"Where did you put it, Marlene?" June Cleaver–firm, taking no nonsense from Beaver or Wally. "That dress is very slimming."

Marlene smiled. "Really? I think it's in the pantry."

All zipped up and on her way out the door, Marlene, dressed to deal with Harry Archer, looked elegant and confident. Ready for *Death Takes a Holiday* and the reception at the Boca Raton Resort and Club. And ready as anyone could be for the Lazarus Society.

Kate could sense Marlene's nervousness; she felt twitchy herself. More creepy than frightened. After all, Marlene would be in a public place and the cryonics crowd might be zealots, but they weren't dangerous. Or were they? That hired thug guarding Life Preserver had gone for his gun. Had he been following Dr. Gallagher's orders?

As they walked from Marlene's apartment to the lobby, Ballou trotting obediently on his leash, Kate said, "We have to stay in touch today," then gave Marlene a kiss on the cheek.

"No problem. If you remember to take your cell phone, I can check in with any news bulletins — like if the Lazarus Society's meeting will be held in the hotel's freezer."

"Very funny, Marlene. Those people are weird at best, so be careful." Kate pushed a stray hair away from her eye. "I'll wear my off-white blazer: I can hide my cell phone in one of its deep pockets."

"Good. But since you're spending the evening with seven murder suspects, you might be the one calling me."

Miss Mitford frowned at Ballou. Marlene and Kate aiming for the rear door ignored her. Outside in the perfect weather, Marlene turned left to the parking lot while Kate and an excited Ballou crossed the pool area, headed for a romp on the beach.

They never made it; Dallas intercepted, waving Kate over to her chaise.

"Hey, sugar, where's your friend, Ocean Vista's Madam President?"

The Texan sat cross-legged, almost in a yoga position. Her blue Capri pants matched the ocean and complemented the sky. She'd tied the tails of a white linen shirt at her waist and tucked her blonde hair under a blue baseball cap. With almost no make-up, Dallas looked younger, fresher. And she seemed less uptight. Less driven.

"Cute dog. A Westie, right? What's his name?"

"Ballou," Kate said curtly, then did an about-face. She had a lot of questions. Dallas could have a lot of answers. "My late husband named him after Ballou, the bear in Kipling's *Jungle Book*. My sons loved that bear, loved that book."

"That's a lovely little story, sugar. So *Chicken Soup for the Soul*. You're an animal lover, then?"

"Yes, I am." Kate smiled, forced, but warm, she hoped.

"My Thistle arrives in town tomorrow, coming all the way from Arizona."

Arizona, wasn't that the site of another cryonics cold storage lab?

192

"And he won't be moving into Ocean Vista. Please pass that information along to your friend, Marlene — actually, she's some sort of kin to you, isn't she?"

"She's my sister-in-law. Many years ago she was married to my husband's twin brother. They divorced, and he later passed away, but Marlene and I are very close. We grew up together."

"Kissing kin. I have lots of them. Over the years, I've grown closer to some friends than to blood relatives. Hell, sugar, I prefer my new Palmetto Beach acquaintances to my old Odessa aunts. Real rattlesnakes."

"It must have been fascinating being married to a cowboy star. Did you meet your husband in Texas?" Kate felt no qualms about prying. Hadn't she shared some of her history?

"Oh, lord, no. I grew up on a farm a few miles from Dallas. I hightailed it out of there just as soon as I'd saved up enough money to buy a bus ticket. It's downright ugly being poor in a city filled with rich folks. I kept waiting tables and taking buses till I arrived in Hollywood. By nineteen-sixty, I was an understudy for Marilyn Monroe."

"Really?" Kate was dying to hear all about Marilyn, but she wanted to stay on point. "Was that how you met Shane?"

"Actually, Shane got the studio to give me that Monroe understudy job. We'd met in the Twentieth Century Fox commissary. I put an extra serving of macaroni and cheese on his plate as he went through the cafeteria line. Though he was the highest paid Western star ever, I didn't recognize him, but I sure thought he looked darling in that Stetson. Anyway, he asked me out to the Brown Derby for dinner and dancing, then invited me to his house for a nightcap." Dallas's voice broke. "I never went home. We'd been married forty-four years when he died."

Kate handed her a Kleenex. Ballou looked up from his investigation of an oleander bush to see if the crying was coming from Kate, then sat quietly when he saw it wasn't.

"Thistle is all I have left now. Such a beautiful horse — the grandson of Shane's first white stallion. I loved all three Thistles, but I raised this colt myself. I'm so glad my baby's coming home to mama."

Could Kate just blurt it out? Dallas was crying again, and Kate, handing her another Kleenex, didn't want to appear insensitive. Oh, well. She *needed* to know. "So, if not at Ocean Vista, where will

194

Thistle be — er — staying?"

The tears stopped. "Why do you ask?" An ice cold delivery.

While Kate struggled to come up with an answer, Dallas stood. "I have a meeting later this afternoon and I want to hop in the shower. I'll see you tonight at Magnolia's." She turned her back on Kate and started toward the lobby door.

Frustrated that Dallas had stumped her, and with Ballou pulling her toward his delayed walk, Kate called out, "Are you going to a meeting of the Lazarus Society?"

Dallas glanced over her shoulder and said, "Nosy neighbors never become kissing kin."

Thirty

"Just how much do you know about the Lazarus Society?"

It was Kate's turn to spin around. "You startled me."

Ballou, who'd been told the walk was imminent, pulled on the leash and gave a half-bark, half-whine. An almost mournful sound, like a basset hound on a bleak moor.

With dancer-perfect posture, red hair blowing in the wind, and her hands on her hips, Mary Frances reminded Kate of Maureen O'Hara challenging John Wayne in *The Quiet Man*.

"Answer me, Kate." Mary Frances's raised voice caused several sunbathers on nearby chaises to sit up and listen.

Shrugging, Kate stole Dallas' line, "Why do you ask?"

"Because the Lazarus Society may be connected to Swami Schwartz's death." She sounded frightened.

Kate softened her attitude and her tone. "Come on, Mary Frances, let's take Ballou for a walk on the beach." The Westie started off eagerly, but kept well away from Mary Frances.

They strolled along the shore, holding their sandals, the lukewarm ocean washing over their bare feet. It felt good. Almost sensuous. Mary Frances's toenails were painted a pastel pink, matching her terrycloth sweat suit. And the rims on her sunglasses were the exact same shade of pink.

She'd have a pedicure. Sunburst Coral. Charlie would approve.

"Are you listening to me, Kate?"

Well, no. Some detective, daydreaming about nail polish colors.

"Sorry. My mind wandered. I'm tired, I guess, but please tell me what's bothering you."

"I met a blind date for brunch this morning. At Charley's Crab, in Deerfield Beach."

What in the world could Mary Frances's love life have to do with the Lazarus Society? Unless? A flutter of excitement started in Kate's stomach and rushed up to her throat. "Did you meet him on lastromance.com?" The words flew out of her mouth. Not her usual laid-back style of wait and bait.

"How do you know that?"

Kate shifted to neutral. "Just a hunch. I think Marlene mentioned you'd tried computer dating. Sorry, go on, Mary Frances."

"Ever since I decided that Joe Sajak wasn't for me — widowers think they're ready to date, but they really aren't — I've been looking. Then yesterday, I received the best e-mail ever. I've memorized it: 'I enjoy fine dining, French wine, and Italian films. You sound like a warm, witty woman, whom I would enjoy getting to know and to share my interests with.'"

Word for word. Harry Archer's e-mail to Marlene.

"At first, he seemed wonderful. Warm, funny, spiritual. He told me about the Lazarus Society — remember, that's the group Dallas Dalton had been asking about on Friday night — whose members passionately believe in life after death. Since I believe in heaven, I thought, despite Dallas, the society sounded great." She sighed. "But then, just as I had my first taste of strawberry shortcake, he started talking about Life Preserver, some medical research lab that freezes dead bodies, and then later revives the patients — that's what he called them — giving the dead a new lease on life. Eternal life. I believe only God can grant us eternal life." Mary Frances shivered in the warm sun. "I'm telling you, Kate, that charlatan took away my appetite."

"Did he invite you to a meeting?"

"No. He realized I was horrified, so he kept trying to sell me on the society, rambling on and on, telling me how the members embrace death, resting assured that they'll be coming back to a far, far better place."

Kate almost gagged. A snake oil salesman quoting the selfless hero of *A Tale of Two Cities*. She patted Mary Frances' arm. "That's awful, but tell me, why do you think the Lazarus Society might be connected to Swami's death?"

"Because, today I learned that Swami Schwartz was a founding member of the society and, like the others, looked forward to his death, so that one day in the not-too-distant future, he would live again in a more technically advanced, more spiritually attuned world. It sounded to me as if some members of the Lazarus Society want to die before their time."

Kate said, "Why hang around if, while your body's frozen, you can work on your soul?"

Ballou tugged on his leash, veering left,

away from children splashing water.

"Right. A few of the more devout want to be frozen as soon as possible, totally accepting that Life Preserver will come up with a cure for whatever kills them, that they'll be defrosted, and will return as better people, living in a better world."

Were the Lazarus Society's members fanatics, putting their faith in mad scientists, willing to die for what they believed in? Oh God! Marlene would be up there at the Boca Raton Resort, mingling with them, watching *Death Takes a Holiday*, getting a price list.

"Your date's name was Harry Archer, right?"

"Are you one of them, Kate?" Mary Frances' shout must have carried to Cuba.

Twenty minutes later, Mary Frances was sipping tea on Kate's balcony.

The dancing ex-nun and Kate had formed an uneasy alliance, swapping information and sharing theories. Ballou had withdrawn to the bedroom.

"So, you, Marlene, and I will band together to ferret out the bad guys, sink Life Preserver, and expose Swami's killer. Like the Palmetto Beach version of *Charlie's*

Angels?" Mary Frances sounded annoyingly perky again.

"More like the geriatric version."

Before she'd put the kettle on, Kate reached Marlene, who'd been waiting for valet parking. Not surprisingly, Marlene refused to abort her mission, pointing out that she'd be safe in the hotel, with its well-trained staff and well-heeled guests milling about, and saying, "No one can brainwash me, Kate."

"Please be careful," Kate had replied, sounding like Marlene's mother. "And call nine-one-one first, then me, if you get in trouble."

"What do you mean trouble? They think I'm a hot — er — cold prospect. What I'll get is a cryonics cost sheet. And be sure and let Mary Frances know that she's not your Dr. Watson. She's only a third banana, on temporary assignment. Ciao."

Thirty-one

Addison Mizner had been at the top of his game when he'd designed the Boca Raton Resort and Club's original structure in 1926, a monument to a fabled era that, like the white outfits on its fabulous tennis courts, had now become history.

Times and fashion changed, but Mizner's coral-pink hotel, a mix of Spanish-Mediterranean, Moorish, and Gothic architecture remained a triumph and the resort's centerpiece.

Today, the Boca Raton Resort and Club's 356 acres included the Cloister, Mizner's original masterpiece, the Yacht Club, the Tower, the Boca Beach Club, the Golf Villas, the Boca Country Club, conferences facilities, two 18-hole golf courses, thirty tennis courts, a 50,000-square-foot spa, a golf clubhouse, six pools, an indoor basketball court, a 27-slip marina, and a half-mile of private beach. And a canopied boat transported guests from the pool, spa, and beach area across the waterway to the golf courses.

Awed, as always, Marlene admired the emerald lawns, tall palm trees, and brilliantly lush purple, magenta, and pink bougainvillea, with the odd jasmine adding scent. The resort smelled as wonderful as it looked.

If she could have afforded one of the villas that came equipped with every amenity known to modern money, plus a beach club membership, Marlene would have moved up here in a New York millisecond. Though Jack Weiss had left her more than comfortable, she'd never live like this, unless, of course, she stumbled over a multimillionaire on the loose in the lobby. From her mouth to God's ears.

The hotel's interior, lots of rich wood and inviting sofas and chairs, charmed her once again, sweeping her back in time to a romance with a tall Texan who'd favored ten-gallon hats and claimed he'd only felt at home in hotels with very high ceilings. The Cloister had more than met his criterion.

"Ah, Marlene, don't you look smart? I love a woman in black." Harry Archer, dressed in crisp khakis, navy blazer, and a school tie, approached her from the right, and reached for her hand. For a moment, she thought he would kiss it, but he only gently squeezed her fingers. "Come along, lovely lady, we're about to start the movie."

She hated to think so much charm could be all con, but when they arrived in the small conference room, where the screen had been set up, her basest suspicions were confirmed.

The other three members of the audience were, like herself, women of a certain age, whose eyes collectively lit up as Harry Archer entered the room. Each of them clearly believed Harry was interested in her — that he was her date — and the others only had been invited to watch an old movie and to learn about the Lazarus Society. Well, if Marlene hadn't been helping Kate play detective, she might have believed that, too.

"Show time!" Harry's megawatt smile circumnavigated the room, lingering briefly, but warmly, on each of his guests. Marlene estimated his too-white implants must have run around fifty thousand. Selling life after death must be a good living.

Which of his four marks would Harry sit next to?

"Unfortunately, I'm a working host, ladies, so I'll sit in the back and run the projector." Harry seemed to have all the answers.

The lights went off, leaving them all in the dark.

Midway through the movie — she'd seen it several times on cable — Marlene's mind wandered. In grainy black and white, a handsome young Fredric March, starring as Death, actually looked like death until he took a holiday. Could that be a cryonics marketing ploy? Freeze frame and rewind.

Sometimes she wished, no prayed, that she could rewind, even for a moment, just long enough to erase her adultery with Charlie. Adultery. Even today, in some countries, women were stoned to death for committing that sin.

A four-martini one-night stand. Well, more like a four-martini fifteen minutes.

She'd take her secret, that terminal guilt to the grave. Charlie had adored Kate. Marlene had loved her like a sister. Yet, they had gotten drunk, flirted at a party, and wound up in bed, on top of the coats, in their hosts' guest room.

Why would anyone want to come back from the dead, to live again, with all your sins intact? Marlene would rather take her chances on an afterlife, where, maybe, she could atone. Or, on nothing, where, finally, she wouldn't remember.

When the lights came on, Marlene went to the ladies room to repair the damage to her makeup. If only she could find a way to repair the damage to her soul.

Thirty-two

Kate brushed on taupe shadow, then decided to line her eyes before applying mascara. That required a magnifying mirror. For some reason, she felt it was important to make a good impression tonight and, when she was tired, soft gray liner opened up her eyes.

Charlie had believed that people paid more attention to well-dressed, well-groomed detectives, gave them more respect. So she'd started early and she'd fussed.

Mindless fussing. Kate always did her best thinking — solving family problems, drafting sympathy notes, planning party menus — while performing mundane tasks that required little or no concentration: brushing her teeth, shampooing her hair, loading the dishwasher, applying makeup.

During this makeup session, she focused on the past, on Swami Schwartz's father's boyhood friendship with Jack Gallagher and Danny Mancini, on Danny being Swami's godfather. Not to mention, Nick Carbone's.

Charlie also believed the past foreshadows the present. Could Swami Schwartz's death be linked to something that had happened decades ago in Brooklyn?

If Danny Mancini were well enough to attend the rehearsal tonight, she'd ask him about his friendship with Swami's father. And what Swami, himself, had been like as a young man, before he'd gone off to India to find himself.

Was any man ever what he seemed? Swami, whom Kate had considered an aesthetic, had convinced his wealthy female admirers in Miami to finance the Palmetto Beach Yoga Institute, had moonlighted by teaching Tantra Workshops, had partnered with Jack Gallagher in the Life Preserver Corporation, peddling cryogenics, and had been a founding member of the Lazarus Society.

Whatever had occurred in the men's past lives, Danny Mancini was plagued with current demons. Debts from his gambling addiction, and, despite his failing health, a lifestyle that could kill him, and an ungrateful godson who'd turned down Danny's desperate requests for money. How easy it would have been for the restaurateur to slip poison in Swami's espresso.

With his partner's death, Dr. Jack Gallagher became sole owner of two corporations. Could greed, one of the seven deadly sins, have been the motive for Swami's death? Gallagher struck Kate as a self-centered, grasping man, but would he have murdered Swami, knowing an autopsy would prevent the yogi from being frozen? From ever coming back? Or had that punishment been the doctor's judgment call?

Lust, another deadly sin, might have contributed to Sanjay's motivation. He wanted Tiffani; she wanted Swami. If Sanjay had spiked the yogi's coffee with cyanide to get the girl, it worked. They'd looked pretty cozy on the beach this morning. And, after Swami's death, as a bonus, Sanjay Patel had been appointed director of the Yoga Institute. Though he'd acted surprised, could Sanjay have been aware that Jack Gallagher would promote him?

Laurence McFee had a screaming match with Swami over his inheritance. Unbelievably, Magnolia McFee had changed her will, leaving most of her millions to Swami for research on what Laurence referred to as a "science fiction project." With the yogi dead, would Laurence be back in granny's will as heir-in-chief? Kate answered her own question: Yes. Why else would young Mr. McFee have threatened Swami?

Somewhere along the way, she'd started to doubt Tiffani Cruz. Just how incriminating were her "sappy" e-mails to Swami? And after he'd spurned those romantic overtures, what had she written in her self-proclaimed "nasty" e-mails? Could Nick Carbone be right? Maybe Tiffani had laced Swami's demitasse cup with poison.

Kate liked Dallas Dalton as a dark horse. That trot around the block just before Swami's death nagged at Kate. Had Dallas left the restaurant to make a cell phone call? To meet someone? Who? She dropped her mascara wand. Hell's bells! Maybe the ubiquitous Harry Archer. Could he have been courting Dallas, too?

Though she couldn't come up with a motive for either Dallas or Magnolia, to-night's memorial rehearsal might open up all kinds of new possibilities. That thought pleased her. Smiling, she grabbed a sponge and wiped the dark brown streaks off the sink.

With her left eye finished, she leaned into the mirror to draw a fine line above her right eye.

The doorbell rang. Who now?

Ballou went wild, as he always did when

he heard the bell. "It's okay, boy." But Kate felt taken care of by the Westie. Mary Frances had left less than thirty minutes ago. It must be someone in the building; otherwise, with Miss Mitford off duty, anyone from the outside would have had to ring her up on Ocean Vista's visitor's phone line.

She opened the door to find Tiffani in tears. Ballou, like all males, hated the sight of crying and went back to his cage in the bedroom.

"I'm on my way home to change, then Sanjay's going to drive me up to Mrs. McFee's, but I had to talk to you." She sighed. "Mr. Mancini disappeared from the hospital, and it's all my fault."

Tiffani, dressed in tight white shorts and a halter — thank God, she was planning on changing — seemed to thrive on the drama, enjoying her role as a messenger delivering bad news. Kate found it difficult to work up sympathy for her, but she was alarmed about Danny Mancini.

She glanced at her watch, then, less than warmly, said, "Come in, Tiffani."

"You were doing your makeup, right?" She pointed to Kate's right eye. "Sorry, this is important, I won't take long."

The girl was astute, Kate would give her

that. "Yes, you caught me in the middle of applying eyeliner. Please make this quick, I have to finish dressing."

"You've always been so nice to me, Mrs. Kennedy, almost like a grandmother. I have no family, you know. My mother walked out when I was six. My grandmother raised me, but she died last year in Kansas City — Missouri, not Kansas. I used the insurance policy money to move down here. You sort of remind me of my grandmother, better dressed, but kind, like her."

A wave of guilt crested, then swept over Kate, still she couldn't shake the idea that she was being conned. "What happened to your mother? Where did she go?"

"Now that's a question with no answer." Tiffani shrugged. "You've got a great ocean view, don't you, Mrs. Kennedy? I'd kill for that view."

Any resemblance to her granddaughters evaporated. "Tell me about Mr. Mancini. Why do you feel responsible for his disappearance?" Kate could hear the coolness in her voice, but Tiffani didn't seem to notice.

"I've screwed up. Big time. Swami told me I was out of line, that he totally wasn't interested in me, that he was old enough to be my father, but I kept chasing him." She sounded like a woman scorned. "Then Mr. Mancini got on my case, told me Swami might not fire me from the Yoga Institute, but he'd fire me from the restaurant. You know I'm paying my own tuition for my associate's degree in massage therapy, I need all three of my jobs. I make the most money at Mancini's. Bar tips. Hardly anybody tips good here at Ocean Vista."

Where was she going with this?

Kate moved into wait mode.

"I resented Mr. Mancini's interference. He accused me of chasing after Swami. At the time I had no idea Swami Schwartz was his godson." Tiffani squeezed her eyes shut. "Yesterday morning at the restaurant, I told Detective Carbone about Mr. Mancini's gambling and how Swami had refused to pay off his debts. I was mad, and, with Detective Carbone throwing all those questions at me, afraid I'd be arrested. Mr. Mancini overheard me and, suddenly, he got sick, almost fainted. That's when Detective Carbone and he left. They might have gone to the hospital."

"Why didn't you tell me all this yesterday?" Tiffani had been lying to her from the start.

"I didn't think you'd help me if you

213

knew what I'd done." She stared at the floor. "And I felt ashamed."

Kate felt ashamed, too. She hadn't gone to visit Danny at the medical center.

"Now Mr. Mancini's run away and Sanjay's looking all over for him. So is Dr. Gallagher. And Detective Carbone. But no one can find him." Tiffani crossed to the balcony and stepped through the open door. "Yeah, that's quite a view."

Thirty-three

Driving his custom-designed, blue — the exact color of his eyes — Jaguar up to Boca Raton, Jack never felt more frustrated in his life. Danny Mancini on the loose, even sick and tired, could be extremely dangerous. Not only to Jack, but to the entire cryonics community.

Where the hell could he be?

Jack had left Life Preserver after the unpleasant encounter with that pushy Mrs. Kennedy and gone straight to Danny's cottage. Since he had a key, he searched it thoroughly. Cluttered. Full of newspapers, Chinese take-out containers, and empty whiskey bottles. No Danny. And no car in his pebbled driveway.

Figuring Danny must have parked his leased Mercedes near the beach this morning before he collapsed, Jack had driven over to the pier and scoured the parking lot and all the side streets in a twenty-block radius. No sign of the black convertible.

When Danny had escaped — no, *escaped*

was too strong a word — run away from the hospital, he must have walked the six blocks back to the beach and retrieved his car. Only sheer determination and lifelong stubbornness would have made that walk possible. Danny Mancini was a very sick man.

Yesterday afternoon and then last night at the medical center's morgue, coming to grips with the autopsy and the horror of that procedure's grisly details, bagging the evidence, marking the vials of blood, and sewing the corpse back together, had added up to the most ghastly day in Jack's life. Today was running a close second.

But he'd survived the worst, hadn't he? He could certainly handle Danny Mancini and Kate Kennedy.

Or could he?

Danny Mancini, a paradox, knew just enough to ruin Jack's dreams. It wouldn't be the first time.

And that nosy Parker, Kate Kennedy, might somehow stumble on the truth. He'd called Jeff Stein to complain about her tactics, but the *Palmetto Beach Gazette* was a weekly paper and its editor hadn't been at his desk on such a beautiful Sunday afternoon.

He'd open the sunroof, but he didn't

want to mess up his hair. Though he had his presentation down pat, Jack had long ago recognized the value of style over substance, and the messenger being as important as the message. Image was everything, especially when explaining cryogenics. He wondered how many prospects Harry Archer had lined up for today's talk. Small groups worked better for first-timers at a Lazarus Society meeting. Jack preferred close encounters with his potential patients. After all, one day he might be frozen alongside them.

Jack wished that Harry, formerly a very successful timeshares telemarketer, whose skills had transferred so smoothly to cryonics, would vary his script. Enough of *Death Takes a Holiday.* Why couldn't he show *Ghost?* That should whet their appetites for a return appearance — of both body and soul.

Or *Topper.* He'd first watched *Topper* while playing hooky almost seventy years ago. Such a charming, classy movie. A movie that had changed his life.

Almost no one knew the truth about his past. He'd done everything he could to erase it. After only a brief reference to being born in New York City, and having attending Groton, his curriculum vitae started with his Yale undergraduate degree.

Swami Schwartz knew. So did Danny Mancini.

But Jack's secret had been kept so well and for so long that not even Nick Carbone, whose father had been some sort of a *paesan* of Danny Mancini's, ever knew Jack had lived in Brooklyn.

On that overcast Tuesday in 1937, he and Danny had skipped out of school right after Sister Margaret Rose's religion class — where she'd taken attendance and they'd stolen two quarters from the mite box — jumped the subway turnstile and gone into the city to the Paramount Theater.

As a straight-A student, he had no qualms about missing school. On the few occasions he'd given it any thought, Jack realized he never felt guilty about anything.

Sitting in the grand art deco theater with starlike lights twinkling in its ceiling, watching *Topper* interact with the elegant ghosts, Marian and George, and listening to their witty dialogue, Jack had made two decisions. He'd get the hell out of Brooklyn. And one day he'd speak like Cary Grant. Realizing those plans would take money, and his widowed mother, who cleaned houses for rich people on Park Avenue, had none, Jack made a third decision: He'd start running numbers for old Sam Schwartz, who'd been the most successful bootlegger in Brooklyn and still ran the biggest bookie operation in the borough.

A woman in a pickup truck cut in front of him, jolting him back to the present peril of navigating I-95.

He blew his horn and she stuck her hand out the window and made an obscene gesture. In some ways his poverty-stricken youth seemed genteel compared to today's vulgar society.

Danny's dad had delivered ice and his mother had worked in the garment district as a seamstress in a men's suit factory. She'd outfitted Danny and Jack in John David rejects, turning Jack into the best dressed mob apprentice in the neighborhood.

How he'd loved running for Sam Schwartz, making money.

Schwartz's son David, a spoiled brat, in Jack's opinion, had been mooning over Rashmi, the daughter of an immigrant from India who ran an import/export business. Their romance had cast a cloud over David's Bar Mitzvah, the best party Jack had ever attended.

That same night the Raiders, a gang of young hoods from Coney Island, having had some success with extortion, petty theft, and bookmaking on their own turf, and wanting to take over Sam Schwartz's, attempted to kidnap David Schwartz.

At thirteen, Jack, already over six feet, lean and tight, had been working out in the YMCA, where he won most of his boxing matches.

When one of the Coney Island kids pulled out a gun and shot David, hitting him in the arm, Danny ducked. But Jack kicked the gun out of the hood's hand before he could fire a second time, grabbed it, and shot the Raider in both legs.

Sam Schwartz had packed Jack and his widowed mother off to Greenwich, Connecticut, with his eternal gratitude and a big chunk of change. The bookie then collected on some favors and Jack found himself enrolled in Groton. The first class he'd signed up for was Elocution.

He'd graduated as valedictorian, then went on to graduate magna cum laude from Yale, and second in his class from Harvard Medical School. And his sainted mother had lived to see most of her son's triumphs.

Practicing medicine with distinction for over fifty years, he'd won too many awards to count. And he'd founded, then served as CEO of the most successful HMO in the United States.

He looked forward to one final accomplishment in these, his twilight years: the Nobel Prize in Science for his work in the field of cryogenics.

Thirty-four

Dr. Jack Gallagher stood behind a podium fielding questions like a forties film idol being interviewed for *Photoplay*.

Marlene would have recognized him anywhere. With that shock of white hair, those incredible twinkling blue eyes and a tan that George Hamilton would envy, he looked even better than he did in his photographs in the *Sun-Sentinel* or in his appearances on the local television news stations.

He smiled warmly, acknowledging her entrance, while not missing a beat in responding to his current questioner, a squat lady swathed in a large patterned, mostly-purple print.

During the less than fifteen minutes that Marlene had been in the ladies' room, crying off, then putting back on her mascara, the conference room had been miraculously transformed. The projector and movie reels had been removed and a table laden with tea sandwiches and eclairs had replaced the screen. The cream-color taffeta drapes were open, letting the sunshine in, and revealing miles of aqua sea. A sexy, sun-kissed waiter holding a silver tray stood behind the table, serving white wine in crystal glasses.

Several more ladies of a certain age and two men, who had to be over ninety, had joined Harry Archer's three recruits. Lazarus Society members in good standing, Marlene assumed. Gallagher's audience sat, a few with straight, posture-perfect backs, some with visible signs of osteoporosis — listening in rapt attention to the squat lady, a new prospect, timidly querying the doctor. Softball questions, lobbed in awed tones.

Marlene couldn't wait until Gallagher's number-one fan ran out of platitudes. Her own interrogation would make Bill O'Reilly seem like a neutered pussy cat.

Whoa — what was she thinking? She had a role to play here. Dual roles, in fact: A convert to cryogenics. And an admirer of Harry Archer. So she couldn't tick off Dr. Frankenstein.

Demurely — or as demure as a tough old New York City broad can appear — she accepted a glass of wine from the surfer hunk, moonlighting as a waiter, and took a seat.

Competing floral-scented colognes filled the room, vying for dominance.

As Marlene fought an urge to gag, the smitten squat lady asked, "Can you explain the process, Dr. Gallagher?"

"Oh yes, and could you please tell us more about where we'll be residing while we're waiting to come back?" Another new recruit in the front row, a tall lady with a blue rinse and a tight perm, gushed out her question.

Before the doctor could respond to either woman, Marlene's hand shot up as if she had no control over her action, no explanation of why any semblance of rational behavior had run amuck, other than the devil made her do it.

With great poise, and no apparent annoyance, Jack Gallagher's bright blue eyes met Marlene's and held her gaze. "You have a question, miss?"

"It's Ms. Friedman, Doctor Gallagher. And, yes, I do."

Smiling with great warmth, he opened his arms, palms up. "Delighted to have you here with us today, Ms. Friedman." He rolled her name around in his mouth as if tasting fine wine, then swallowed. "Fire away."

"When will we come back?" Marlene

hesitated, not sure of her ground. "I mean, is there a game plan? Next month? Next year? Next century?"

"When?" He repeated, sounding pleasant, but puzzled.

"Right. When?" She raised her voice. "What's the ETA for our resurrection? For our recycled bodies to return to life. Should our heirs keep paying the maintenance fee on our condos?"

A woman behind her gasped in disapproval. One of the old men hissed; it whistled through his false teeth. Marlene certainly wasn't winning over any friends in the Lazarus Society.

"That's a most intriguing question, Ms. Friedman." The doctor chuckled, softly. "If you three lovely ladies will indulge me, I promise to address all of your questions."

He might have missed a cue, but Jack Gallagher was back on script now.

"A brief history, if I may. Until recently, death, unlike Fredric March in the movie, never took a holiday. We died; we were buried. Case closed. And no matter what our religious persuasion, even those of us who believed in a final judgment, where our souls would reunite with our bodies as the faithful rose into heaven, ever would have imagined in our wildest dreams that it might be possible for our dead bodies to return to health and to live again here on earth."

Marlene duly noted the "might." Jack Gallagher sounded like a Yale-educated Elmer Gantry, selling something better than salvation: Immortality. However, she also heard undertones of Jim Jones and shuddered, remembering the hundreds of men, women, and children who'd died in South America following the preacher's order to drink Kool-Aid laced with cyanide.

Convinced that Kate's theory about Swami Schwartz's death being connected to both Life Preserver and the Lazarus Society was correct, Marlene now wondered, could Swami have quarreled with the doctor over his vision moving too fast? Going too far?

In his commanding, yet melodious, upper-crust accent, Jack Gallagher carried on. "Though the cryonics movement began in 1962, an association promoting cryogenics wasn't formed until 1967. I joined immediately. All these decades later, based on the pioneers' and my own extensive research, I founded the Life Preserver Company to provide South Florida with the finest cryostasis research and testing in the entire country. Our ultimate goal, in addition to our ongoing lab work, is to offer the best treatment available anywhere in the world: careful screening of prospective patients, rapid on-the-spot worldwide care when needed — our patients may not die in South Florida, but we'll be ready to assist them wherever and whenever necessary, the most sterile vitrification preparation in the industry, followed by outstanding and compassionate long-term patient care, with the finest quality of cryopreservation, using state of the art suspension in liquid nitrogen."

Still holding his audience captive, Gallagher paused to take a sip of water.

It occurred to Marlene that Harry Archer's other prospects seemed far better clued-in to cryogenics, and in possession of far more information, obviously, having gone through a much deeper indoctrination than she had. For her, listening to Dr. Gallagher's lecture was like joining a class halfway through the semester.

But then, she'd aborted her conversation with Harry in the Breakers before he'd completed his sales pitch. Maybe she could channel her abrupt departure and her lack of knowledge into an advantage, inviting Harry to give her a private cryonics lesson over an intimate dinner. Hell, she'd even offer to treat.

She caught up with Dr. Gallager mid-sentence. "And we regret that some small rodents must die, but our research, primarily with stem cell testing and tissue transplants, requires sacrifice, so our human patients may live again."

Jack held up a colorful brochure. "One lovely lady inquired about the cryonics process. It's fully explained here. In brief, I like to think of vitrification as the polar opposite of embalming. A second lady asked where the patients are housed. I rather like that image, I consider the freezing and suspension process as a long sleep, from which the patients will awake, fully cured. And Ms. Friedman wanted a time frame, an ETA."

He nodded at Marlene, eyes bright, expression sincere. "That, my dear, is anyone's guess. Science could catch up next year or, as you suggested, many years from now. Consider cryonics as an insurance policy. If you go into a grave or are cremated, you'll have no chance of ever coming back. If you opt for suspended animation, you'll have every chance. And that's why I suggest the family plan, so you'll return to life with people you know and love."

The audience burst into applause.

"Enroll early to reserve your spot. Our costs, starting at 120,000 dollars for a full-body suspension, are more than competitive."

And what would he charge to freeze a head without its body?

"In some cases, a patient requires premedication. Most don't. What is of paramount importance is retrieving the body promptly after death and beginning the vitrification process as soon as possible in a controlled, exceedingly cold temperature, applying the fluids carefully, taking care not to crack any tissue. It's never good to keep a cryonics patient at high temperatures even for a short time, a special concern here in Florida. All transportation to our Life Preserver lab and our satellites abroad will be in temperature-controlled ambulances. For now, Life Preserver will preserve and freeze our patients, then transport them to another storage area. We're totally prepared for longterm suspensions, and soon, we'll be ready to accept and house patients here in Palmetto Beach, while science catches up and finds a cure for whatever caused their deaths."

"Damn straight, sugar. You'd better be

ready. Your first long-term-care patient arrives tomorrow." Dallas Dalton had joined the Lazarus Society's meeting.

Thirty-five

The usually well-behaved Ballou peed on a leg of the couch. Kate sighed. She'd never get her other eye done.

"You're a bad boy, Ballou."

The little Westie lowered his head, his ears drooping.

Should she give him a time-out? Put him in his cage-bed? Show him who was calling the shots around here?

No, maybe he had another bladder infection like the one he'd suffered from after Charlie had died. She'd planned to take Ballou for a walk just before leaving for Palm Beach, why not do that now?

She ran into the kitchen, filled an old Tupperware bowl with warm water and ammonia, then wiped off the couch and the carpet. The dejected dog watched as she raced around.

Finished with her mop up, she washed her hands, grabbed her sunglasses — she'd do the other eye when she returned — her keys, a plastic bag, the pooper-scooper, and Ballou's leash. He yelped and jumped, trying to lick her hand. "Stop that, I'm still mad at you. Now, come on, this is going to be the shortest walk of your life."

Lifting him up, no easy trick, Kate carried the Westie through the lobby, even though Miss Mitford had gone off duty. "See, we obey the rules, Ballou. Good people carry their pets through the lobby. And good dogs don't pee on the furniture."

Ballou licked her cheek.

She headed for the front door. No walk on the beach. Since she didn't want to return windblown and sandy, this brief outing would take place on A1A.

The brightness of the late-afternoon sun startled her. She moved her sunglasses from the top of her head to the bridge of her nose. Better. She turned south toward Fort Lauderdale. Cars buzzed by, their noise an intrusion on the pedestrian-free boulevard. Kate and Ballou seemed to be the only ones out there to enjoy the light breeze, the scent of jasmine, and the rustling palms.

They walked at a fair clip for the equivalent of two city blocks, Ballou evidencing no interest in a bush or a tree or stepping off the curb to do his business. Contrary, wasn't he?

Like Danny Mancini. Where had that stubborn old man gone? And why hadn't she gone to visit him in the hospital? What could have happened to him? Had someone gotten into his room? Had a phone call lured him away? Was his disappearance linked to Swami's death? It must be. But how? Could Dallas have been right? Had Danny poisoned his own godson? She doubted that. Had he run away? Or had he found out something that scared him off? Any chance he'd show up at Magnolia McFee's tonight?

She blinked back a tear. Could Danny be dead, too?

If her theory about Life Preserver and the Lazarus Society being connected to Swami's death was correct, how did Danny Mancini fit into that scenario?

And if Jack Gallagher had killed Swami, it couldn't have been to keep his master plan a secret. Dallas, Magnolia, Laurence, Danny, probably Tiffani and Sanjay, not to mention Jeff Stein and herself, all knew that Gallagher wanted to freeze, store, and revive the dead on premises. Even the town council had questioned if Life Preserver might, eventually, be providing more than just research. Good heavens, the egomaniacal doctor was taking reservations, selling storage space.

Greed worked as a motive, but Gallagher had tons of money. Did he really *need* total control of another company?

What about his past? Past secrets often lead to present problems. Where had he grown up? And where had he acquired that Mid-Atlantic accent? The who, what, where, when, and why scoop. How she loved those details. Maybe she should consider Jeff Stein's job offer.

According to Dallas, Swami's father, David Schwartz, and Danny Mancini had been best buddies in Brooklyn, tough guys, hanging out with gangsters, and they'd served together in World War Two. Could the secrets — or the sins of Swami's father and godfather — have been festering for over sixty years?

Should she call Danny's other godson, Nick Carbone? His parents might have talked to him about the old days.

"Are you carrying a baggie, Kate?" A Brooklyn baritone, slightly mocking. "I'd hate to have to arrest you and Ballou for littering."

Kate started. Could she have conjured up Nick Carbone? Spinning around to confront him, her sunglasses fell to the sidewalk.

Carbone, agile for a man with a belly the size of a beach ball, kneeled, retrieved them, paused to pet a happy-to-see-him Ballou, then handed Kate her glasses. "What the hell is wrong with your right eye?"

Charlie used to tease her, saying she looked like a white rabbit without her mascara and liner.

She felt herself flush, waving her sunglasses about before putting them back on. "Nothing, I mean, I didn't finish." Why was she explaining makeup interruptus to Nick Carbone? "Nothing's wrong. What are you doing here?"

"I came to see Mrs. Dalton, but she's not home. I called the Ritz-Carlton, but she's not in her suite there, either. As I was leaving Ocean Vista, I spotted you and Ballou. Any idea where I can find the Yellow Rose of Texas?"

Did he find Dallas attractive? As Kate flushed again, her neck went hot. Why the devil did she care what — or who — he liked? She didn't. She wouldn't even care if he wanted to date that flashy Texan. She wouldn't. Yet, somehow, she did.

Breathing deeply, she said, "Dallas will

be at Magnolia McFee's memorial rehearsal tonight."

"Yeah, I heard about that." With a deep laugh, he added, "The very rich are different from you and me."

So he could quote Fitzgerald.

"I thought I'd catch her." He glanced at his watch.

Should she test him? See how much he knew. What he'd figured out. Sure, why not?

"Dallas might have stopped at the Boca Raton Resort on her way up to Magnolia's. To attend a meeting of the Lazarus Society."

"Okay. If you're still playing detective, Miss Marple, I'll play straight man. How did you hear about the Lazarus Society?"

Oddly annoyed that he'd called her Miss Marple — she wasn't that old and he wasn't all that much younger than she — Kate said, "Palmetto Beach isn't so different from St. Mary Meade. People talk."

"People?"

"Do you know a man named Harry Archer? He's hawking memberships in the Lazarus Society." She hesitated, catching a look of what — surprise? — respect? — in Nick Carbone's brown eyes, then added, "I think the society's a support group for Life

236

Preserver's cryonics business."

He nodded. "I'm warning you Kate, stop snooping. Harry Archer is more than a sleazy, former timeshare telemarketer with a new scam selling eternal life. One old gal he'd courted up in Palm Beach County died under suspicious circumstances, but the Lantana police didn't have enough evidence to arrest him. He was tried last year in Margate for bilking another old lady out of her life savings."

"Why isn't he in jail?" Good God, Marlene planned on interrogating this guy. Kate, as usual, had left her cell phone home. She had to cut this conversation short.

"The jury, mostly women," Nick almost, but not quite, sneered, "found him not guilty."

"I have to get ready for Magnolia's rehearsal, but I have a quick question for you."

"You don't know when to quit, do you, Kate?"

Hearing an iota of grudging respect in his voice, she plunged. "I gather you haven't found your godfather yet."

It was his turn to flush, going scarlet from his neck to his forehead, tiny beads of sweat dancing down his cheeks.

"Go color in your other eye, Kate."

"Do you know where Danny Mancini is?" She knew she'd crossed the line.

Carbone glared at her. If he'd meant to unnerve her, he succeeded. Still, she tried again. "Family secrets can destroy us, Nick. In some way, we're all victims of our pasts, aren't we? I'd like to help."

Ballou tugged on his leash, wanting to move forward. And, to Kate's amazement, Nick patted the top of her head, pivoted like a cadet, and went the other way.

Thirty-six

"Everything's just fine." Marlene was whispering. Kate had called, in her June Cleaver, mother-knows-best mode, and Marlene, in the middle of luring Harry Archer down to Miami for dinner, didn't have time for a lecture. She glanced over at Harry and, still whispering, said, "Keep your phone on, I'll call if I need you to send in the Marines."

After his audience of aging bobby-soxers had mobbed Jack Gallagher as if he were the second coming of Sinatra, the doctor swept Dallas Dalton off into a corner where, apparently, they'd come to a truce. The Texan then joined the other newcomers filling out applications for membership in the Lazarus Society.

Marlene had pulled Harry aside and invited him to dinner. Probably smelling a Life Preserver enrollment and — no doubt, with its $120,000 price tag, a hefty commission — he'd readily accepted, suggesting Palm Beach. A half-baked plan was hatching in her head, and wanting Harry as far away from Palmetto Beach as possible, she had countered with South Beach. They'd been discussing their options when Kate called. Ever polite, Harry had walked a few feet away, but Marlene suspected he was eavesdropping.

"A jealous ex-boyfriend," she said, by way of explanation, while snapping her cell phone shut. "I'd never want to be frozen with him."

"And I don't much want to be frozen with you." Dallas appeared at Marlene's side. "Cryogenics makes for mighty strange roommates."

"Well, maybe you can be stabled with your horse."

Harry, employing what closely resembled a cha-cha step, backed away from them. "Dr. Gallagher appears to be ready to leave, ladies. Please excuse me for a moment."

While Dallas struggled for a retort, Marlene went for the kill. "Where's your husband, Shane, frozen? You've never mentioned that. Isn't he on the Life Preserver family plan with you and Thistle?"

Dallas's perfectly madeup face sagged, her chin almost resting on her chest. "How dare you?"

"We're going to be late for Magnolia's command performance." The unflappable

Gallagher reached for Dallas' elbow. "Come along now, I'll drive." Right behind the doctor, Harry nodded in approval.

"The hell you will. Get your hands off me, Jack, I'll drive myself." Dallas whirled around and left the room, a panel of white chiffon floating behind her, not unlike Loretta Young's dramatic exits on her old TV show.

Gallagher sighed. "I'm afraid you touched a nerve, Ms. Friedman. Shane Dalton decided to be frozen and suspended in Arizona next to his first wife, whom he'd divorced decades ago to marry Dallas, and who passed on last year shortly before Shane. Their only son will be a patient there, too, when his time comes. So you see, Shane did have a family plan, only Dallas wasn't on it."

Marlene bit her lip. "I gather Dallas inherited the horse when Shane died."

"Indeed." Gallagher sounded grave. "And Dallas and Thistle will be frozen, suspended, and return together."

Marlene smiled, picturing Dallas and Shane Dalton in a future-life cryonics custody suit, but said nothing.

The Lazarus Society meeting officially over, the doctor, with Harry at his side, led his followers out of the conference room.

On their way down the corridor, Gallagher turned to Harry. "Small crowd tonight."

"But very passionate." Harry came across as defensive. "Three of the prospects enrolled on the spot. And I'm going to have dinner with Marlene Friedman."

Did he think she was deaf? Or could Harry be so self-absorbed he didn't realize that she and the squat lady were only a few paces behind him and the doctor?

"What happened to the former nun?" Gallagher sounded puzzled.

Harry shrugged, his broad shoulders rising to his ears, making his thick neck disappear. "She canceled. Said being frozen conflicted with her belief in life after death in heaven, where, when this world ends, her body will again host her soul for all eternity."

Omigod! Harry was talking about Mary Frances. Well, good for the dancing nun, he hadn't conned her.

"That's so foolish. So sad." The doctor said. "Poor uninformed woman. Why would anyone allow faith to get in the way of cryonics? Passing up on the chance to be frozen and suspended, gambling on eternity in heaven? Didn't you explain that cryogenics is the most spiritual branch of science. Your former nun has missed out on the Lazarus Society. On becoming part of Life Preserver's community, part of our core cell of cryonics patients who'll come back together, body and soul, to live again in a brave new world."

Marlene shivered.

"What's the matter? It's not cold. Aren't you feeling well, Mrs. Friedman?" The squat lady, who obviously hadn't been straining to hear Jack — he spoke softly — and Harry's every word, sounded solicitous.

"I'm fine." Marlene, still eavesdropping, cut her off.

"By the by, Harry, thanks again for helping me out at the morgue Friday night. I could never have pulled this off without you."

"My pleasure, Doc. Did Nick Carbone take you at your word?"

"Certainly. Why wouldn't he? Am I not the most respected doctor in South Florida?"

Jack Gallagher *was* Dr. Frankenstein. Life Preserver *was* his lab. And Harry Archer *was* his henchman.

Thirty-seven

Kate could count the number of times she'd ridden in a chauffeured limousine. To weddings and funerals mostly. New Yorkers took taxis, not limos, to special events, as well as when it rained, when running late, or when the Madison Avenue bus didn't come. She and Georgie Cooper, too short by far to slow dance with, had hailed a taxi to her high school prom. Some of her classmates in their pastel, full-skirted, tulle gowns had hopped on the subway, the IRT's doors barely wide enough to accommodate those multiple layers of crinolines.

Kate missed the city's ubiquitous yellow cabs. But maybe, in South Florida, limousines were easier to come by than taxis. This one was white, sleek, and roomier than many a Manhattan studio apartment.

Tonight, she felt almost festive in her silvery gray pants suit, with an antique silver and green brooch on its lapel that, according to Charlie, flattered both her hair and eyes. And she'd finally finished making up her right eye. Nick Carbone's face flashed into the picture, complicating her feelings, compromising her memory of Charlie.

Mary Frances opened the built-in mahogany bar. "Look, my favorite. Macadamia nuts. Should we have a drink?"

The array of bottles, from Remy Martin, to Moët, to Johnny Walker Black, along with the proper crystal, from brandy snifter, to flute, to highball, to hold your drink of choice, impressed Kate. "Sure. How about champagne?"

Wearing a green silk shirt and matching high-waist, wide-leg trousers, reminiscent of a thirties movie star's loungewear, Mary Frances had bounced into the lobby with a surprisingly upbeat message, "Let's go get the bad guys."

Since they were on this mission together, why not toast its success? And Marlene's success with Harry Archer.

Kate reached for the Moët, then tackled the cork.

"Champagne would be perfect." Mary Frances sniffed. "Doesn't the leather smell wonderfully rich? A girl could get used to this."

The pop exploded like a shot. Even the driver jumped. Kate always had assumed the glass between a limousine's front and the backseat was soundproof. She wondered if Magnolia McFee — or maybe her grandson, Laurence — had instructed her chauffeur to spy on them. And that thought didn't strike Kate as paranoia. Quite the contrary. Whispering, she warned Mary Frances.

As they talked about nothing, Kate pressed a button and her window opened. Sipping champagne, she gazed up at the sky. Gathering clouds in a dusky blue sky, and, from beyond the horizon, a glimpse of a rising pale moon. So beautiful, it seemed unreal. Like a postcard. Or a paper moon hanging over a cardboard sea.

Winding their way up A1A's two-lane highway, they arrived in Palm Beach, with mansions to their left on the much wider Intercoastal side, and the ocean to their right. As always, Kate marveled at how narrow the beach strip was on this tony, pricey island. Just enough space for a couple of draped Arabian tent-style cabanas and a few beach chairs. Not much sand for the billionaires to kick around.

Mar-a-Lago loomed ahead, its pink and coral buildings sprawling over acres behind high hedges. Kate said, "Since Magnolia McFee is Donald Trump's neighbor, we should be there any minute."

Sure enough, as she spoke, the chauffeur turned left through Calvary Cemetery-size, black, wrought iron gates. A circular driveway, flanked by Royal Palm trees, so tall that they blocked the waning daylight, ended at a white antebellum mansion, with wide pillars and a verandah with swinging settees. Emerald-green grass sloped down to the Intercoastal. Magnolia trees and a huge weeping willow graced the lawn. What a setting. Where were Scarlett and the Tarleton twins?

A ramrod straight, unsmiling butler in a charcoal-gray cutaway and striped trousers opened the door. "Welcome to Seacrest."

Though she'd read about Merrywood and Hickory Hill, and had gone on tours through Mount Vernon and Monticello, this would be Kate's first time as a guest in a house that actually had a name. And a snobby butler with a British accent. She wished Marlene could be here.

"Mrs. McFee awaits you in the drawing room. Follow me, please." Kate stared in awe at the center hall double staircase, fully expecting to see Rhett standing on the top step, wowing the local belles. Behind her, Mary Frances giggled. Why had Kate allowed her to have a second glass of champagne?

In the drawing room that seemed as large as Ocean Vista's lobby, floor-to-ceiling French doors opened out onto a terrace with stone steps leading down to a dock. The requisite yacht, this one a sloop, was berthed next to a cigarette boat. The latter, probably one of Laurence's toys, seemed appropriate for a scion of a Winston-Salem tobacco family.

"That's a real Picasso, not a print," Mary Frances whispered, gesturing toward a painting hanging over a pale yellow sofa. "His blue period. I took an art appreciation course at the Palmetto Beach Senior Center last year."

Sanjay Patel sat across the room on an identical yellow sofa with Tiffani Cruz, in a too-tight, too-bright mini dress, huddled so close to him that their thighs touched. A Rembrandt hung above their heads, but they only had eyes for each other.

Were they the only ones here?

Magnolia McFee, dressed in a Lily Pulitzer pink and green-print cotton shift and a pink cardigan sweater, stepped out from behind an armoire that could have hidden a basketball team.

"How lovely to see you again, Mrs. Kennedy. Miss Costello." She crossed the room, grabbing hold of Kate's right and

Mary Frances' left hand for a fleeting moment. A firm grip for such a frail old lady. "Cocktails are being served on the terrace." Then glancing with distaste that bordered on hostility at Tiffani and Sanjay, Magnolia said, "Please come along now. We need to get started." Her words cold as cryogenics.

Laurence McFee, in a navy blazer, white linen shirt, khakis, and Bally loafers without socks, stood behind the terrace bar stirring an oversize martini. He nodded cordially at Kate and Mary Frances, then handed the cocktail to Magnolia. "Your favorite, Grandmama."

Kate, not wanting anyone mixing her drinks, asked for a Diet Coke.

Laurence served her in silence, then opened a bottle of white wine and poured a glass for Mary Frances. Wine from a freshly opened bottle should be fine, but Kate would forbid Mary Frances from accepting a second.

"Excuse me, ladies, I want to take this Scarlett O'Hara down to Dallas." He placed a ghastly looking concoction on a silver tray. "She's having a stroll in the English garden."

An English garden in South Florida soil? Money must be a powerful fertilizer.

Magnolia sighed. "I'm going in to collect Sanjay and Tiffani. No sign of Danny Mancini. Poor soul. But everyone else is here. Jack Gallagher and Dallas Dalton were fussing, so I packed him off to the library to select an urn for Swami from my Indian art collection. You wouldn't believe the ugly reproduction Jack brought for the memorial. I'm sure Swami wouldn't have approved, either. This is all too depressing, isn't it?"

A rhetorical question, Kate presumed, as Magnolia turned her back and walked toward the drawing room.

Could Swami's ashes be in the doctor's urn? Kate's heart thumped faster and her stomach lurched. She reached into her pocket for a Pepcid AC, washing it down with Diet Coke. How had Gallagher completed the autopsy so quickly? And, more important, with an ongoing police investigation, how could Swami have been cremated so soon after he'd died? And on a Sunday?

"Stay here, Mary Frances." Kate pointed to a copper-color rattan chair. "I'm going to talk to Dallas."

"But I want to help."

"We need to separate. Ask Tiffani and Sanjay a few questions. Try to find out

250

when their romance really started. And, for heaven's sake, don't have any more wine. One of these people poisoned Swami."

"What about food? Surely we can eat."

"Only after someone else has sampled whatever you're thinking about having."

Maybe Mary Frances wouldn't make it, even as a third-banana detective.

Kate crossed the terrace, went down the stone steps, and turned left, walking into the English garden via an arched trellis of magnificent yellow roses.

In an alcove filled with beds of foxglove and a statue of Pan, Laurence was nuzzling Dallas' neck, not seeming to care that she was old enough to be his mother with decades to spare. Dallas moaned, then leaned back in his arms as he worked his way up to her lips.

Thirty-eight

"A lot of motives for murder are going around, Charlie." Standing alone on the end of the dock, staring out across the water like Jay Gatsby, Kate spoke aloud. Her one-sided conversations with Charlie had tapered off, but hadn't ceased. She prayed they never would.

The cigarette boat rocked in the evening breeze that had picked up considerably since they'd arrived at Seacrest. She looked up at the sky. The clouds were turning gray and the temperature had dropped, too. A gathering storm.

"Laurence might have two motives: A dead Swami couldn't be Granny Magnolia's biggest heir or the wealthy Dallas' lively suitor."

But was Laurence only after the Texan's money? Their romantic performance in the garden would belie that theory. He and Dallas had been so enthralled, so enamored during the interlude that neither of them realized they had an audience.

"A penny for your thoughts." The soft,

refined voice coming from behind made her lurch. "They may be worth much more. Should I up the price?" A hand clutched her shoulder. "Careful, Mrs. Kennedy, you wouldn't want to fall in, would you?"

If a threat, the doctor had caged it in dulcet tones.

With a burst of courage, what Charlie used to call spunk, she stiffened her spine, straightened her shoulders, and spun around, pleased that her movement made Gallagher lose his grip.

"Good evening." She smiled warmly. "You're just the man I wanted to see."

"Oh?" His soft voice lacked curiosity. Almost a foot taller, he stared over her head at the water, not sharing her enthusiasm or meeting her eyes.

"Yes," she sounded perkier than Mary Frances flirting with the widower, Joe Sajak. "You have such excellent taste, Dr. Gallagher, and, despite what Mrs. McFee says, I'm sure that the urn you selected and filled with Swami's ashes is wonderful. But I'm so interested in East Indian art. Would you show me which one of Magnolia's urns Swami will be spending eternity in?"

He blinked, then swayed for a second,

seemingly speechless.

Bingo! The doctor *had* brought the ashes with him.

The breeze became a wind, whipping the cigarette boat against the dock, blowing Kate's hair into her face. Raindrops pelted the back of her silk shirt.

"I understand you volunteered to perform Swami's autopsy, that must have been very difficult for you." Even as she spoke, Kate sensed she was missing something. The real motive. The truth. The secret. The Life Preserver link — she had to find a way to get into that lab. "You must have finished up the autopsy late last night. And then made special arrangements to have the body cremated today. Fast work, Doctor."

They stood there, getting wet, playing a waiting game.

When he finally spoke, he sounded strangled. "You're wrong. I only offered to do the autopsy after Nick Carbone told me the medical examiner, Horatio Harmon, had gone on holiday."

Kate, thinking how convenient it would be for a murderer to perform an autopsy on his own victim, heard Charlie's voice prompting her. "Or maybe you knew the coroner would be away."

The butler, carrying the biggest black umbrella Kate had ever seen, came running. "Please come with me. Mrs. McFee needs both of you straight away, she's about to start the rehearsal."

An off-white canvas canopy had been rolled down and now covered the entire patio. Food, drink, and guests were dry. Except, of course, for Kate and Dr. Gallagher.

Mary Frances sat in the same rattan chair, holding a china plate heaped with Chinese food. Fried rice. Spare ribs. Egg rolls. Sweet & sour sauce. It looked like take-out. Maybe the very rich weren't so different after all. Kate could only hope Mary Frances had waited for a food-taster before digging in.

Dallas and Laurence stood at the bar, sipping Scarlet O'Hara cocktails. For him to down that god-awful mix of grenadine and Southern Comfort, the man must be seriously smitten.

Alone at a small round table, Sanjay munched on an egg roll, his eyes fixed on Tiffani who stood in the center of the patio giving a dreadful reading of the Twenty-third Psalm. In front of the French doors, Magnolia waving a Bible, yelled, "Stop!"

The butler handed towels to Kate and

Jack. "May I bring you some hot tea?"

"Thanks. That would be lovely." Kate dried her hair. Her gray silk outfit was toast.

"Sir?" The butler addressed Jack Gallagher.

"Yes, and put a shot of brandy in it."

"Tiffani, perhaps you'd do better with St. Paul." Magnolia spoke with no conviction.

Hearing a rustling sound, Kate glanced toward the shrubbery and spotted Danny Mancini moving gracefully along the edge of the patio, using one hand to balance a tray above his head, looking very much like the waiter he once had been. And he was wearing expensive, if damp, new clothes.

"*Regardez*," he shouted, sounding intoxicated. "I have here two bottles of cyanide that I found hidden in Magnolia's azalea bushes." Then he tumbled into a potted palm.

Thirty-nine

"Aren't you glad I lured you here?"

"You bet. I've never been lured to dinner by a lovelier lady." Harry clicked his martini glass against Marlene's. "Here's to South Beach."

He locked eyes with her momentarily, then went back to ogling the passing parade of scantily dressed nubile women — their roller blades covered more skin than any other item of their clothing — skating down Ocean Drive. Marlene had never seen so many belly buttons in her life, but she couldn't fault Harry. She'd been admiring the sexy topless guys showing off their sculptured muscles. The ocean, lighted by that famous moon over Miami, served only as a backdrop for these beauties.

Ah, youth. Even in her prime, Marlene hadn't been nearly as confident, healthy, or striking as the current crop of young people and, in truth, she couldn't remember any subsequent generation who'd topped this bunch.

Sitting on the sidewalk at a postage stamp–size table, they literally could have reached out over the outdoor café's low wooden railing and touched the skaters. She'd bet more than one customer had tried.

"Is the food as great as the ambience?"

Though she tried not to, Marlene laughed. Harry's eyes were locked on a diamond stud in a sixteen-year-old girl's navel, but his voice didn't hold a trace of irony. No doubt he expected Marlene to consider his question a compliment.

"Is something funny?"

Oh God, to think that only yesterday, she'd found this jerk attractive.

"Everyone comes to Rick's." She forced a smile. "For both the lobster and the atmosphere." She wondered how Harry would react if he knew she was planning to steal his car.

Fate had stepped in, and her half-baked plan to sneak into Life Preserver emerged fully hatched. All because of a valet parking ticket.

After she'd easily sold him on South Beach, Harry, himself, had suggested they take his car. He'd be happy to drive her back to Boca, "no problem, dear lady," he

258

lived very near the hotel. When he'd turned in his ticket and paid the fee at the Boca Raton Hotel's valet parking desk, Marlene noticed that Harry carried every key he owned on the ring with his car key. One of them would open the door to Life Preserver.

All the way to Miami, in his black SUV, she'd said very little, just kept nodding, smiling, patting his hand, and plotting.

Rick's had valet parking, too. And, because there were no parking spaces on the strip, the restaurant charged a bloody fortune. Harry had turned over his heavy key ring, put the ticket in his blazer pocket, and complained about the cost. Marlene had smiled and said, "I told you this would be my treat. And that includes the parking. So hand over that ticket, sir."

Now all she had to do was wait for him to go to the men's room.

"Another martini, Harry? Or would you prefer a tall glass of water?"

Sipping his second martini — she'd passed, knowing she had to remain alert — he started his sales pitch, going into great detail about the core cryonics group coming back together, often stealing word for word from Jack Gallagher.

Over the excellent jumbo shrimp cocktail, Marlene asked sweetly, "What happens if a patient opts to only have her head frozen?" She tried to sound sappy. "Do you think, by the time we return, science will have found a way to clone new bodies from our DNA?" She smiled. "If so, I'd like to be thirty pounds thinner."

"Wouldn't we all?"

Nature called between the appetizer and the main course.

Harry excused himself, leaving his blazer draped over his chair. Men made notoriously short pit stops. She didn't have much time. But the blazer beckoned. She grabbed it, quickly rifling through the pockets. If Harry had no money, no cell phone, and no car, he'd be in a real pickle, wouldn't he? Couldn't pay the bill. Couldn't call his boss. Well, he could, from a pay phone: Collect. She'd bet he hadn't memorized Jack's cell phone number. No one actually knew their friends' or colleagues' numbers. They just programmed them in. Dropping his wallet and cell phone into her bag, she calmly walked into the restaurant proper, then exited through the front door. No one seemed to notice that she'd skipped out on the bill. Of course, if their waiter had noticed, he'd assume that Harry would be paying. She almost wished she could hang around and watch the fun.

Marlene never thought she'd be sitting in the driver's seat of an SUV. These gas guzzlers should be banned. She hadn't wanted to raise the valet's suspicions by fussing around, trying to adjust the seat, so here she sat, way too high off the ground. Nonetheless, she was barreling up I-95, heading for Palmetto Beach. She'd pull over at the first rest stop and call Kate. She couldn't wait to tell her about their upcoming breaking-and-entering caper.

Forty

"Don't touch that!" Kate, trying to reach Nick Carbone on her cell phone, shouted as Laurence McFee stooped and reached for one of the bottles that had rolled under a table. "Those cyanide bottles are evidence."

"Planted to make me look guilty!" Laurence screamed. "Everyone knows those azalea bushes are my turf."

Not everyone. It was news to Kate. She'd never have pictured Laurence as a gardener, digging around in dirt.

Jack and Sanjay lifted Danny out of the bushes and were helping him into a chair.

Magnolia wept softly. She collapsed into a rattan rocker, appearing ashen and frail.

Kate said, "Sanjay, you might want to check Mrs. McFee's pulse."

The butler arrived with hot coffee before anyone thought to ask.

"I'll stick with my Scarlett O'Hara," Dallas said, though she hadn't been offered anything else. She swayed slightly, then clung to the bar.

Tiffani, who seemed to be in shock, suddenly stood and bolted out of the room.

Kate turned to Mary Frances who, to her credit, was gently applying a cold cloth to Danny's head. "Can you please find Tiffani? Make sure she doesn't try to leave."

Sanjay jerked his fingers away from Magnolia's throat. "What are you saying, Mrs. Kennedy? You sound as though Tiffani has reason to run."

"Nick Carbone." The detective's voice boomed in her ear.

"Danny Mancini's here at Magnolia McFee's. He arrived with two bottles of cyanide that he'd found in her azalea bush, then collapsed, but he seems to be coming around. Should I call the local police?"

"No need, I'm right outside, Kate. We had an all points bulletin out on Danny. I was on my way to the Palm Beach police station to check out Harry Archer's rap sheet when one of their patrol car drivers recognized Danny's license plate and called me. So here I am, along with the officer who spotted him. Tell your hostess to open up the gates."

Mary Frances returned with a sullen Tiffani in tow. When Sanjay tried to talk to the girl, she literally pushed him away, walked over to the bar, and poured a jigger of gin, which she downed neat.

Kate wished she had a sweater. The night air had turned chilly. Cold. Her head ached, not to mention her stomach. So much happening here — her thoughts wouldn't stop racing around, always coming back to Swami Schwartz's murder and Life Preserver's mission. What if . . . ?

Danny struggled to his feet as the butler led Nick and a young, Latino police officer onto the terrace.

What if . . . ? What if the ashes in Jack's urn weren't Swami's? Oh, God! How crazy was that?

"Kate, I'm speaking to you." Nick Carbone didn't sound remotely cordial.

"Sorry." Embarrassing. Since she couldn't tell him what she'd been thinking, she fell silent.

"I apologize for my bad behavior, I shouldn't have crashed into the party like that." Saving her from having to say more, Danny inched toward Nick. "But I'll bet those cyanide bottles belong to Swami's killer." He spun around, surprisingly agile for a sick man, and pointed his index finger at Laurence. "Bang, bang, Flower Boy."

An hour later, Nick was driving Kate and Danny back to Palmetto Beach, and

Mary Frances was following them in Danny's car.

The young policeman had bagged the cyanide bottles. Danny had apologized for skipping out of the hospital, explaining that Jack had been driving him crazy, but he felt much better now. And, no, he wasn't going back to any hospital. Nick had warned everyone if prints were found on the bottles, he'd be asking all of them to come to the Palmetto Beach Police station tomorrow to be fingerprinted. An ugly end to the still-weeping Magnolia's rehearsal.

Now, from the backseat, Kate asked Danny, "Where did you go?"

"I got out of the hospital without anyone asking me a question. Then I walked back to the beach, got my car and drove up to the Ritz-Carlton."

"Really?" Kate tried not to laugh. "The Ritz?"

"Well, Jack told me I'd been left some real money in Swami's will. So I checked in, ordered room service, had a gourmet lunch, and bought myself some new duds. Great shopping at the Ritz, Kate. I spent the afternoon at the pool, had a sauna, and decided to show up for the rehearsal."

"How did you get in?"

"When the gate opened for Dallas, I

drove in right behind her. Parked over to the side. Thought I'd nose around. Swami had told me about fighting with Laurence over Magnolia's will. I figured that poor excuse for a man might have murdered my godson. Looks like I was right."

Her cell phone rang. It could only be Marlene, so she had to take it.

"Hello."

"I have the key to Life Preserver and we're going in. Where are you?"

Kate gulped. "Er . . . just crossing into Broward County. I'm with Nick Carbone; we're driving Danny home."

"There's no time to spare. Ditch them. Have Carbone drop you off first at Ocean Vista. I'll be there in fifteen minutes."

Forty-one

They'd passed through Deerfield Beach before Kate mustered the courage to put Marlene's plan into action. "Nick, I'm really tired. Could you please drop me off first?"

"Didn't you hear me tell Mary Frances to go straight to Ocean Vista? I'm going to stay overnight at my godfather's. We'll come by and pick up his car tomorrow."

How easy was that? Kate felt a twinge of guilt, but it vanished under an avalanche of anxiety. She and Marlene would never get past Life Preserver's armed guard that easily. Unless . . . they had a decoy. Something to distract him. What? Maybe a damsel in distress? Did she dare ask Mary Frances? She certainly could play the role to perfection. But would the former nun agree to take part in an illegal search? Since they had a key, their caper wouldn't really be considered breaking and entering, would it? Though she tried to swallow it, a nervous giggle escaped.

"Having a good time back there all by yourself, Kate? If I didn't know better, I'd think you were up to something." No laughter in Nick's voice.

To distract him, she went on the offensive. "What about Dallas Dalton? Did you ever find out why she walked out of the restaurant just before Swami was poisoned?"

It was Danny who answered. "Dallas went out the front door, then returned through the back door and popped into the ladies' room, right? It's her Saturday night ritual, Kate. Kinda like going to Mass on a Sunday."

"A ritual?"

"Yeah. See, her horse, Thistle, died on a Saturday night at nine o'clock. So every Saturday at nine p.m., wherever she is, Dallas goes outside to bay at the moon or some such damn fool thing. She told me Thistle was a Scorpio rising, whatever the hell that means."

Knowing Dallas, the truly weird ritual somehow made perfect sense. And Kate had pretty much eliminated her as a suspect anyway.

Mary Frances stood in front of the lobby door. She'd beaten them to Ocean Vista and must have put Danny's car in a guest parking spot.

As Kate hopped out of the backseat, Nick leaned across Danny and said,

"Please, no more detective work tonight, Kate. I'll call you in the morning."

A strange black SUV pulled up behind them.

"Of course I'm in. Justice must be served. Harry Archer should be punished. What do you want me to do?" Mary Frances sounded eager and appeared unflappable. Kate bet she'd allowed her students to get away with murder.

"Okay," Marlene said, "bold as brass, you drive my old Caddy convertible right up to Life Preserver's door. Use your considerable charm to get the guard to help you. Tell him you're lost."

"Why would I be in an industrial park this late on a Sunday night?"

Dallas baying at the moon came to mind, but Kate said, "You took a wrong turn, you've been going around in circles, you're hopelessly lost. Get him to drive you back to the gate."

"Kate and I will be parked a few warehouses away. When you and the guard drive off, we should have more than enough time to find out which key opens the door."

"Then what?" Mary Frances sounded dubious.

Kate said, "He'll have to walk back. That's about six city blocks, I'd say. We'll be inside by then." She hoped. "You drive east, park a few feet away from the gate, turn off the engine, and wait for us. We'll ditch the SUV and ride home with you."

"Won't the guard notice that Life Preserver's lights are on?" Mary Frances asked.

Marlene pulled a small flashlight out of the SUV's glove compartment. "Courtesy of Harry Archer, we're prepared."

The moon was way too bright for sneaking around. Marlene and Kate huddled on the far side of a home furnishings warehouse three buildings removed from Life Preserver, peeking around its corner. They'd parked the SUV with the company's vans behind the warehouse.

"Okay, let's move out!" Marlene pointed, as her Caddy passed by, the guard at the wheel.

They were at Life Preserver's door in less than thirty seconds.

Yanking the key ring out of her pocket, Marlene sighed. "Did you ever see so many bloody keys?"

"Does this help?" Kate focused the flashlight on the key ring.

"Yes, hold it steady." Marlene tried one, two, three, four keys, struggling, but failing to get any of them to fit into Life Preserver's two locks.

"Complicated. Damn." She tried a large silver-tone key, "Bingo. One to go."

How much time had elapsed? Kate's heart raced. "Hurry!"

"What the hell do you think I'm doing?"

She inserted a small oddly shaped key and the second lock opened.

They stepped into a pitch-black room. Behind them, the heavy door closed with a thud. Kate prayed the guard hadn't returned yet.

Marlene shone the flashlight rapidly around the room. An attractive reception area with dark drapes on the windows. Two doors were dead ahead.

"The lady or the tiger?" Marlene asked.

"I choose door number one."

"You sound like a contestant on *Let's Make a Deal*."

On the sixth key, the steel door opened. A strange aroma greeted them. The room was icy cold.

"Keep the light on the floor!" Kate was feeling her way along a steel wall.

"No one can see us in here." Marlene's voice trembled. "I found a switch."

Light filled the room. They were in a high-tech lab: cold, sterile, terrifying. Suspended from the ceiling directly ahead of Kate, a rectangular cylinder, sort of a cross between a glass-paneled coffin and a steel curio cabinet, swayed. Inside, close enough to touch, was the frozen, nude body of Swami Schwartz. His head seemed to defy gravity and float in front of her face. She screamed.

Marlene dropped the flashlight. It rolled across the marble floor.

Jack Gallagher stepped out from behind an empty cylinder enormous enough to hold a dead horse. Kate saw madness in his blue eyes.

Trembling, he pointed a gun at her. "You're trespassing on sacred ground," he shouted. "I'm calling the police."

Not exactly what Kate had expected.

Epilogue

Dr. Jack Gallagher was guilty of many things, but not murder.

Swami Schwartz, fanatically eager to go down in history as the first cryogenically frozen body to be brought back to life, and diagnosed with a fast-spreading brain tumor, committed suicide with a little help from his friend.

They timed Swami's suicide to coincide with Palmetto Beach Medical Examiner Horatio Harmon's vacation, so the good doctor could jump in and perform his friend's autopsy. He had no fear of inhaling secondhand cyanide, knowing that Magnolia McFee always carried a mask.

When Swami's body had arrived at the medical center late on Friday night, Gallagher, with henchman Harry, whisked Swami — now the doctor's "patient" — out of the hospital morgue and off to Life Preserver to administer vitrification and cooldown. On Saturday, Gallagher falsified the autopsy reports, using research animal tissue. On Sunday, a John Doe, who'd died of natural causes at the medical center, went to the crematorium and his ashes were placed in "Swami's" memorial urn.

Gallagher had planted the cyanide bottles in the azalea bushes to frame Laurence, hoping that Magnolia, who'd reserved prime cold-storage space, would then leave her many millions to Life Preserver.

Monday morning, the doctor faced numerous criminal charges ranging from operating without a mortuary license, to tampering with a police investigation, to medical malpractice.

Harry was arrested as Gallagher's accomplice and co-conspirator and agreed, after a conversation with Nick Carbone, to drop his grand-theft-auto charge against Marlene.

Monday afternoon, Dallas met Thistle's van and, at great expense, shipped him back to Arizona. She and Laurence would move there, too, just as soon as Dallas could buy her way out of Ocean Vista. Magnolia planned on dissolving the Lazarus Society and, in what might turn out to be the world's weirdest extended family, would be living with her grandson and Dallas.

In a history-making decision, a Broward County judge granted Sanjay permission to transport Swami Schwartz's frozen remains to the Arizona cryogenics facility.

Monday night at Mancini's Restaurant, Danny, looking great, poured the finest champagne in the house. Dallas, Laurence, Magnolia, Tiffani, and Sanjay, along with Mary Frances, Kate, and Nick hoisted their flutes to toast Swami.

Marlene raised the martini she'd ordered straight-up.

On ice was not an option.